S0-AEQ-337

THE MAN TAMER

BY
CINDI MYERS

® MILLS & BOON®
Pure reading pleasure

*First published in Great Britain 2008
by Harlequin Mills & Boon Limited,
Eton House, 18-24 Paradise Road, Richmond, Surrey TW9 1SR*

© Cynthia Myers 2007

ISBN: 978 0 263 86202 7

14-0408

*Harlequin Mills & Boon policy is to use papers that are
natural, renewable and recyclable products and made from
wood grown in sustainable forests. The logging and
manufacturing processes conform to the legal environmental
regulations of the country of origin.*

*Printed and bound in Spain
by Litografia Rosés S.A., Barcelona*

CINDI MYERS

adores chocolate-covered strawberries and is a fan of professional indoor lacrosse. She lives in the mountains of Colorado with her husband and two dogs, and has not succeeded in training any of them.

For Becci

1

Why Man Taming Works
Dear Man Tamer:
You are so full of it! I can't believe you're telling all these women they can train a man like a dog. How could you ever believe your so-called methods would work on a real man?
A Real Man

Dear Real Man:
The Man-Taming principles work because they're based on tried-and-true methods of Behavior Modification. Behavior modification has been used successfully for decades for everything from, yes, dog training to helping people quit smoking. And it works for helping men break the bad habits they've developed over the years, too. I have hundreds of letters from satisfied readers to prove it.
The Man Tamer

RACHEL WESTOVER'S second-most favorite thing in the world was chocolate-covered strawberries. Since her *most* favorite thing wasn't something she could do in public, she was happy to see the strawberries prominently displayed on the buffet table at Denton Morrison's annual brag party. The media mogul and all-around rich guy made it a point to throw a party for himself every year to celebrate his accomplishments and to show off his latest project for the press.

Rachel's plan for the evening was to corral Denton at some point and ask him—again—about her proposal to fill the vacant slot in the afternoon local programming block of KTXK, the television station he owned. After all, as the most popular columnist in the history of *Belinda* magazine—another Denton Morrison holding—it was time she expanded her audience to television. Chocolate-covered strawberries were the perfect fuel to prepare her for her encounter with "Mr. Money" Morrison.

Anticipating that first luscious bite, she transferred three of the largest berries to her plate. They were the size of eggs and coated in dark chocolate. *Yummmmmm.*

"Have you talked to him yet? What did he say?"

Rachel looked up from the strawberries to her best friend, Moira Stapleton, who was hurrying toward her from the other end of the buffet table. "Did he say yes? Did he give you the afternoon time slot?" Moira asked as she skidded to a stop in front of Rachel. Five foot two inches, with a cloud of dark curls and Bambi eyes, Moira reminded Rachel of a nervous poodle.

"I haven't talked to Denton yet. I'm working up the nerve." She nodded to her plate.

Moira's eyes widened. "*Oooh,* those look yummy. And fattening." She pressed her lips together, resisting temptation. Moira lived off black coffee, water and sushi, and it showed. She wore a size zero. If she weren't so much fun Rachel might have been tempted to snap her in two like the twig she was.

Moira rose up on tiptoe and scanned the crowd. "Have you seen David? He was supposed to meet me here."

"I haven't seen him, but I just got here myself." David Brewer was an accountant at Morrison Enterprises and Moira's erstwhile boyfriend.

"You don't think he's going to stand me up again, do you?" Deep worry lines formed above Moira's nose. "He's so absentminded. He'll get to working on his car or watching a game and the next thing you know, he's forgotten all about me."

Rachel thought a man in love ought to be more considerate than that. What did it say about the depth of his feelings if replacing spark plugs or counting touchdowns could make him forget his soul mate? "Have you been trying any of my techniques?" she asked.

The worry lines deepened. "I tried, but I guess I'm not very good at discipline. I mean, he looks at me with those big brown eyes and I melt. I just want to be with him, you know?"

"I know." Rachel patted her friend's shoulder. "But remember, you're the woman. It's up to you to set the tone for the relationship. And those techniques have been proven to work. Do you still have the list?"

"Yes." Moira opened her purse and began digging through it. She came up with a crumpled computer printout. "One, teach by example," she read. "Two, praise good behavior. Three, distract from bad behavior. Four, substitution—replace bad behavior with something else. Five, reprimand bad behavior. Six, withhold affection until he behaves properly. Seven, punish bad behavior. Eight, restrict unwanted behavior. Nine, reward good behavior, and ten, acceptance—a last resort." She looked up at Rachel. "Maybe I'm at number ten. I mean, you can't really change people, can you?"

"Behavior modification isn't about changing *him*," Rachel said. "Only the way he acts."

"Isn't that the same thing?"

"Of course not. He'll still be the man you love, only better."

Moira stuffed the list back into her purse. "I don't know. I mean, this man-taming stuff may work for some of your readers, but maybe every man doesn't respond to this kind of thing."

Rachel shook her head. "I don't believe that. You just have to keep working at it."

"No offense, but if they work so great, why are you still single?"

Rachel had heard the question so often now she didn't even flinch. "You know why. Since my Man Tamer column became so popular, I can't find a man who'll risk dating me." If she was lucky enough to find a guy who hadn't heard of her column, after a date or two one of his friends tipped him off and he disappeared.

Not to mention so many of the men she met were so, well, *bland*. They were handsome, professional, with money and manners and plenty of opinions, but with no real spark. Where were the debonair, charming and sophisticated men with polish *and* personality?

The last guy she'd dated had even accused her of being too cool—but what did he expect when he did nothing to raise her temperature?

"Men don't want to be tamed," Moira said. She grinned. "They're all afraid of you."

"It's just the name of my column. It doesn't mean I go after men with a whip."

Moira giggled. "You might try it sometime. Some guys really go for that sort of thing." She leaned in closer and lowered her voice. "Your sister's here."

Rachel flinched. "Where?" Rhonda Westover Mac-Millan—Mrs. Harrison MacMillan—could never forget her role as big sister, which to her way of thinking gave her carte blanche to run Rachel's life.

"Over by the door to the terrace. With that group of men."

Of course Rhonda was with a group of men. The hairier sex had panted after her ever since she was a toddler in ruffled panties in nursery school, where she would bat her eyelashes and little boys would vie to share their afternoon animal crackers with her.

Rachel studied her sister now as she held court over five men in black suits, like some lounge singer with her backup group. Clinging close to her side was Harrison MacMillan himself, fifteen years older and many times richer than Rhonda. But of course, all that money was Rhonda's now, and Rhonda made sure plenty of it was spent on keeping up her fabulous face and figure, not to mention endowing numerous charities and throwing lavish parties, all of which served to keep her name in the paper as one of Dallas's most famous socialites.

Which explained what she was doing at Denton's big shindig. The two ran in the same circles, though they weren't exactly friends.

What would Rhonda say when little sister had her own television show? Rachel wondered. The first time a member of the public recognized Rachel before Rhonda, big sister would have to buy out Nieman Marcus to assuage her wounded ego.

Frankly, Rachel couldn't wait.

"Are you going to go over and say hello?" Moira asked.

Rachel shrugged. "I wouldn't want to interrupt." Besides, Rhonda was sure to seek her out, if only to offer some bit of sisterly wisdom. Last time they'd met, Rachel had endured a lecture on the evils of cheap shoes. Never mind that they were at a backyard barbecue. Rachel had worn a pair of funky flip-flops, decorated with rhinestones and feathers. Rhonda, tee-tering on silver high-heeled sandals, swore her little sister was going to ruin her feet or—worse—get a repu-tation for being tacky. "I'm sure we'll bump into each other sooner or later." But not if Rachel could avoid it.

Moira was no longer listening. She was staring toward the door, her expression lightened. "There's David. I'll catch up with you later."

She darted off after her man, leaving Rachel alone with her strawberries. The chocolate had softened a little on her plate, but that would make them all the more decadent.

She lifted a fat berry by the stem and shut her eyes. Her mouth closed over the treat and she took the first bite, sweet juice and velvety cocoa mingling in her mouth. She moaned a little at the positively orgasmic mix of luscious strawberry and rich, smooth chocolate.

"Excuse me, waiter," said a masculine voice at her elbow. "I'll have what she's having."

Rachel's eyes snapped open and she stared at the man who'd interrupted her moment of indulgence. Tall and muscular, he managed to look rough-around-the-edges in spite of his tailored blue suit. His gold-streaked brown hair needed a trim and the stubble along his chiseled jaw testified to the fact that it had been a few days since he'd used a razor. He smelled of expensive aftershave and leather, an intoxicating combination even though he obviously wasn't Rachel's type. She preferred someone more sophisticated, less…rugged.

Of course, right now rugged didn't sound so bad. She was a woman who hadn't had a serious relationship in fourteen months, two weeks and three days. But who was counting?

"Don't let me stop you," the man said in a definite Aussie drawl. "I'm quite enjoyin' the show."

Rachel managed to swallow the rest of the bite of strawberry and looked for somewhere to stash her plate for safekeeping. Whether it was the warmth of the room, or the heat that had swept through her upon locking eyes with the gorgeous Neanderthal in front of her, chocolate had melted all over her fingers and was running down her hand. "Where are the napkins?" she asked.

"Don't see any," the hunk said, not bothering to look around. His blue eyes telegraphed his amusement at the whole situation.

"There have to be napkins somewhere!" She looked around, frantic. The chocolate was in danger of dripping either onto her white silk dress or the white Berber carpeting. But of course there wasn't so much as a cocktail square anywhere in sight.

She was debating wiping her hands on the white linen tablecloth when the hunk spoke up again. "Might be I can help."

Before Rachel could protest, he took hold of her wrist and brought her fingers to his mouth. As she gaped at him, he began *licking* the chocolate from her fingers.

She froze at the first touch of his tongue and stared at him, heart pounding. Was this guy for real? They didn't even *know* each other and he was taking these kinds of liberties. Worse, as his tongue caressed her skin she began to feel weak in the knees and seriously turned on.

How pathetic was it that a total stranger could make her this hot? Granted, he was a gorgeous specimen who practically oozed testosterone, but if she hadn't been so socially deprived of late surely she would have told him where to get off instead of melting into a puddle at his feet like this.

In the meantime he kept licking the chocolate from her fingers. Hot velvety tongue gliding over sensitive nerve endings, sending sparks of sensation traveling through her until her whole body practically quivered. She wanted to steady herself with her free hand on his broad, muscular shoulder, but she was powerless to do anything but breathe hard.

When all the chocolate was gone he released her and they stood staring at each other. He looked almost as dazed as she felt, and as his gaze continued to bore into her she became aware of a warm flush washing over her cheeks. Here was a man who had definitely raised her temperature—too much. She had important business to think about this evening. She couldn't afford to be distracted by a good-looking stranger—no matter how lust-worthy.

"I—I can't believe you did that," she stammered, tearing her eyes away from him and attempting to regain her composure.

"Must be the champagne." He took a step back and raked a hand through his hair, only succeeding in adding to his sexy, just-rolled-out-of-bed look. "Where's a decent beer when you need one?"

Rachel eyed the plate of strawberries, wondering if she dared risk finishing them. She really *needed* chocolate about now. Maybe when Mr. Gorgeous left…. "I think there's a keg in the corner," she said.

He made a face. "Not that American piss. I mean a *real* beer."

The conviction in his voice almost made her laugh. "Let me guess—you mean an *Australian* beer."

"Accent gave me away, did it?" He grinned. His middle upper tooth was slightly crooked, as if it had been knocked loose at some point and never quite fixed in place. Rachel's stomach fluttered. Since when had crooked teeth been sexy? Obviously, since now.

"Who *are* you?" she asked. Despite the suit, he didn't remotely resemble the usual cadre of executives associated with Denton Morrison.

"Name's Garret Kelly." He offered his hand. A large, warm hand that engulfed hers. His grin widened. "Oops, feels like I missed a spot." He held up her hand for inspection. "There it is, right by your thumb."

Before she could protest, he bent his head low and drew her thumb into his mouth. This time, she did brace herself with a hand to his shoulder. She was dimly aware she was losing it badly—losing her dignity and focus and all those things she prided herself on. But she couldn't seem to help it. Brash, brawny Garret Kelly—and his amazing tongue—had positively bewitched her.

He was doing more incredible things to her with his tongue when an all too familiar voice boomed in her ear. "I'm glad you two are getting to know each other, but do you think you could contain yourselves until you're alone?"

Rachel jerked her hand from Garret's grasp and jumped back, bumping into the buffet table, china and crystal chiming. "Mr. Morrison! This isn't what you think!"

With his shaved head, single gold earring and suit tailored to hide his paunch, Denton Morrison resembled a genie turned corporate kingpin. Now he was grinning like a genie wacked out on fairy dust. "I think it's perfect!" he chortled. "The press will love it."

Rachel's stomach sank to somewhere around her knees. Not a good sign that Denton was so gleeful. The only thing the billionaire liked better than money was publicity. She didn't want to think what kind of angle he'd play with her and this Aussie Adonis. She glanced at the plate of strawberries longingly. What she wouldn't give for another chocolate fix—alone.

Garret kept a grin fixed on his face while stifling a

up again when they could be alone and really get to know one another.

TEACH BY EXAMPLE, praise good behavior, distract... substitute...reprimand...withhold...punish...restrict... reward...accept. Rachel's advice played over and over in Moira's head like a bad radio jingle. By the time she reached David she was sure the smile she gave him was strained. "Hi, sweetie," she said, standing on tiptoe to kiss his cheek. "I'm glad you made it."

"Yeah, well, I figured I'd better put in an appearance."

"You look great," she said, brushing a bit of lint from the shoulder of his sport coat. The fabric stretched across his muscular body. Though not too tall, he still had the stocky build of the football lineman he'd been in high school. A little heavier around the middle, but still very attractive, she thought.

He accepted a glass of champagne from a passing waiter and started across the floor toward the buffet table, Moira in his wake. "Let's grab some food and mingle a little, then we can bug out. The Stars drop puck at eight. I'd like to at least get home in time for the second period."

Hockey. Moira rolled her eyes. Lately, David's idea of a hot date was an evening on the sofa watching sports. They could cuddle during commercials, but otherwise interruptions were not welcome.

At the buffet, David filled a plate with food while Moira tried to figure out which of Rachel's principles to use. She'd already praised him for showing up. Distraction?

"I thought maybe tonight we could do something different," she said. "There's a new club over in Deep Elum. The band is supposed to be great. I know you like discovering new music."

"Yeah, but not on a hockey night." He scowled at her. "You know me better than that."

Did she? When they'd first started dating, David had been a fun, attentive companion. He could always make her laugh with his dumb jokes, and he'd proved to be a sensitive lover. But lately he'd taken her for granted. As if he'd grown so comfortable in her presence he no longer had to make any effort to improve their relationship.

"Hey, is that Garret Kelly?"

"Who?" She looked up to find David pointing across the room. "Where?"

"The big guy over there by the keg. That *is* him. Let's go meet him." He grabbed her hand and tugged her across the room.

"Who is Garret Kelly?" she protested, dragged along like a dinghy towed by a yacht.

"Only the best indoor lacrosse player in the country. Led the league in goals last year when he was with the Denver Mammoth."

Sports again. Moira groaned.

They reached the group by the keg. "Hey, I'm Dave Brewer." Dave stuck out his hand. "I'm a big fan of yours."

"Pleased t'meet you, Dave." Garret turned his smile on Moira. "And who is this lovely lady?"

Moira stood straighter and resisted smoothing her hair. Talk about a gentleman….

"That's Moira," Dave said. He scarcely glanced at her before turning his attention once more to Kelly. "I heard the Dallas Devils signed you. That's terrific. I can't wait to see you play."

"I'm looking forward to it," Garret said. He smiled at Moira again. He had a nice smile. Sexy even, if you liked the big, brawny type. "Moira, do you know everyone here?" he asked.

She shook her head. None of the people in the circle looked familiar to her.

"These are some of the other players on the team. This chap on my left is Bud Mayhew. Next to him is our goalie Tate Maguire and his wife Leslie. Then Guy Clifford, Slate Williams and Peter Rutherford. And of course you know Dave."

Right. Dave who was all but ignoring her. The others smiled and murmured hello.

"Love those shoes," Leslie Maguire said. "You'll have to tell me some good places to shop around here."

"Don't do it, I beg you," her husband said. "I'm already reduced to one little section of the closet."

"There's always the spare bedroom," Leslie said meaningfully.

"Fine, shop all you want," Tate conceded. "Just don't make me go with you."

"I know what you mean." David inserted himself in the conversation once more. "Moira's always after me to take her to the mall. Why women think men would be interested in that kind of thing is beyond me."

Moira frowned at him. She almost never asked David to go shopping with her. In fact, she could think of nothing worse than having a whining man tagging along while she was trying on shoes. She turned to Leslie once more. "I'd love to go shopping with you one day," she said. "And you should meet my friend Rachel. She's about your size and has great taste in clothes."

"Rachel Westover?" Garret Kelly froze in the act of raising a beer to his lips. "You know her?"

"Sure. She's my best friend." Moira braced herself for yet another comment about Rachel's man taming column.

"Just met her tonight. Over by the buffet table." He took a sip of beer. "Interesting woman."

"Yes, Rachel is very…interesting." And she must have made quite an impression on Garret Kelly. Moira subtly checked him out. Nice suit, but no tie. Definitely the rugged, athletic type. Definitely not Rachel's preferred sort of date, but there was something to be said for a man's man.

Was he man enough to stand up to the Man Tamer? Moira chuckled to herself. Could be Rachel would finally meet her match. No doubt the battle would be fun to watch—from a safe distance.

2

Men and Sports
Dear Man Tamer:
My boyfriend loves sports. Sometimes I think he loves them more than he loves me. He is always going to games or watching them on television. Our entire social calendar is planned around baseball, hockey, football and basketball season. Now he's talking about taking up golf! What can I do to save this relationship?
Hates Sports

Dear Hates Sports:
This is a tough one. For many men, sports are like a religion. They identify with teams and players and are invested in the outcome of games. But these are only games and the trick is to show the man in your life how much he is missing of real life—i.e., a relationship with you—by being so involved in sports. I suggest you start by attempting to distract him by planning fabulous evenings alone. Favorite foods and hot sex are usually winning distractions. Some women have had success

in learning to love sports and sharing them with their men, but if you do this, I suggest insisting he meet you halfway and learn to love movies or ballet or whatever your passion is. After all, a relationship is a partnership. You shouldn't do all the work. In the end, you may have to confront him with an ultimatum. Does he choose sports or you? If he chooses sports, your heart may be broken, but at least you won't have wasted your life on someone who couldn't give you the love you need. Let me know how it goes!

The Man Tamer

RACHEL WATCHED Wild Man Kelly's departure. Her fingers still tingled from the touch of his tongue. Her breasts felt heavy and aching, and the dull throbbing in her groin testified to how fully turned on she'd been within mere seconds of first laying eyes on him. He'd had her so under his spell that if he'd suddenly laid her back on the buffet table and begun stripping off his clothes she wouldn't have protested.

She shifted and squeezed her thighs together, breathless at the thought of herself laid out among the chocolate tarts and cream puffs, a half-naked Garret looming over her.

He'd certainly lived up to his nickname so far. If she didn't have serious business to discuss with Denton, she wouldn't have minded getting to know Garret better. Not that he was at all her type, but he would probably be fun for a fling—provided he didn't get too wigged out by her occupation.

"What did you want to talk to me about?" Denton asked. "I haven't got all evening."

Denton's prompt pulled her back to the present. "Have you made a decision on the afternoon slot on KTXK?" she asked.

"No. I've got a chance to buy the rights to reruns of *Space Cadet Coeds.*"

"*Space Cadet Coeds?*" Was he for real? "I've never heard of it."

"Number one in Japan last year," he said. "I think it'll be a big hit."

"Who's going to watch a Japanese import when they can have a hometown star?" She drew herself up to her full five feet six inches. "The Man Tamer is the number-one relationship column in the state," she said. "A Man Tamer television show would draw the coveted twenty to forty-year-old female demographic, plus it would increase readership for my column."

Denton waved away her words as if he was brushing off a pesky fly. "I'm also thinking about filling that slot with a show all about lacrosse. If would be a great way to build interest for the team."

"You said yourself lacrosse is already hot. Why would you need a show about it?"

"Lacrosse is something that appeals to both men and women. Especially with a star like Wild Man on the team. Who's going to watch your show but a bunch of women with man troubles?"

Only every woman in the city, if you put it that way, she thought. In her experience, every man was some kind of trouble. "So what if the show mainly appeals to women?" she asked. "That's a lot of viewers. Not to mention with my training in psychology and the strong following I already have with the magazine, I could be the next Dr. Phil."

Denton looked pained. "Rachel, you apply dog-training techniques to handling men. It's a cute concept for a column, but I just don't see it translating to television."

"It's not dog training!" she practically shrieked. Noticing half a dozen people turn to look at them, she sucked in a deep breath and tried to remain calm. "My columns promote the use of proven behavior modification techniques."

"Dog training," Denton repeated.

"Call it what you want, but it works. I have hundreds of letters from satisfied readers who've tried my man-taming techniques and transformed their relationships."

Denton looked thoughtful. "So you're telling me you can take any man and turn him into the perfect *tame* boyfriend using your techniques?"

"Of course."

"Even someone like Wild Man Kelly?"

She glanced toward where Garret was standing by the keg, surrounded by half a dozen admiring men and women. He stood with one hand in his pocket, the other holding a plastic cup, a casual, slouching pose. The too long hair, beard stubble and general demeanor spoke of a quintessential bachelor who didn't care much about his appearance. No doubt his apartment was a sty and his idea of a balanced meal was a slice of pizza in one hand and a beer in the other. Hundreds of women had written to her about similar men in their lives.

"I've seen worse." Of course, none of *those* men had managed to reduce her to a whimpering mass of hormones within two minutes of meeting her.

"Then maybe we can make a deal."

"Huh?" She blinked at Denton, coming out of her lust-induced fog.

"I'll make you a little bet." Denton actually rubbed his hands together, a gesture she had never seen outside of a B-movie. "You apply your man-taming principles to Garret Kelly to *tame* him and if you succeed, you can have your show."

"That's fantastic!" In her elation, she almost hugged Denton, but restrained herself just in time. "This will be the easiest bet I ever won."

"Don't count on it," Denton said. "Kelly's got way too much testosterone in his system to tame." He chuckled. "I don't call him Wild Man for nothing. And from what I hear, that applies to both on and off the field."

She glanced toward Garret again. A short brunette was beaming up at him, her expression telegraphing the message, *Take me, I'm yours.* So maybe Wild Man wouldn't be a pushover. No one ever said she didn't like a challenge.

"I can handle the Wild Man," she said, a thrill running through her at the thought. Okay, so she'd like to *handle* him in more ways than one. All in good time....

"Denton, how marvelous to see you!" Rhonda, her timing impeccable as always, descended on them in a perfumed cloud. She offered her cheek to Denton, who obligingly kissed her. Rhonda made a show of just now noticing Rachel's presence. "Hello, Rachel. I didn't know you were here."

"Of course not. Why would you notice little old me?" She took a step closer to Denton, in an attempt to keep him from being completely lured away by Rhonda's black-belt charm. "Denton and I were just discussing our plans for a television show based on my Man Taming columns."

She ignored Denton's frown and kept her gaze fixed on her sister.

Rhonda's smile vanished, replaced by an expression more appropriate for funerals and firing squads. "Oh no! Please tell me you aren't going to embarrass yourself—not to mention the rest of the family—by taking these ridiculous ideas of yours public."

"Hello? I write a monthly column with a circulation of over two hundred thousand. I'd say that's pretty public."

"The Man Tamer is one of *Belinda* magazine's most popular features," Denton said. His defense of her pleased Rachel, though she suspected the billionaire just liked pitting the sisters against each other. The socially acceptable equivalent of female mud wrestling.

Rhonda's expression didn't lighten in the least. "I suppose reality television and daytime talk shows prove the general public has a taste for sensationalism," she said. "Still, it's difficult to accept that a beloved family member would lower herself so."

Only Denton's presence and fear of making a public scene saved Rachel from slapping her sister. She forced a saccharine smile to her face. "Just think of it as my way of helping people to get the most out of their relationships," she said. "I know how interested you are in philanthropy." Rhonda was on the board of half a dozen Dallas charities—not because she was so interested in the underprivileged, but because it kept her name and face in the spotlight.

"Speaking of charity…" Rhonda latched onto Denton's arm and fixed him with a dazzling smile. Rachel thought about telling her to lay off the teeth whitening. It was starting to look a little scary. "I wanted to discuss the upcoming fund-raiser for the Children's Hospital…." Ignoring Rachel, she steered Denton away, a determined tugboat towing a not-so-reluctant barge.

Rachel headed back toward the buffet table and a fresh plate of strawberries—and a pile of napkins. She was going to drown her frustrations in chocolate and plot her next move with Garret Kelly. A positively evil smile shaped her lips as she pictured herself, on Garret's arm, introducing him to Rhonda. "This is Wild Man Kelly," she'd say. "The star of the Dallas Devils and my *very* good friend." One older husband—no matter how wealthy and socially prominent—wasn't a match for a muscular hunk with a sexy foreign accent. Rhonda would be positively green. A good color on her, Rachel thought.

"MEN LIKE GARRET KELLY think they're happy living the way they do, but that's only because they don't know what they're missing." The following Monday, Rachel stirred sweetener into her iced tea and eyed Moira across the café table. "I can show men like him how to improve their lives."

"For your sake, I hope it involves regular sex," Moira

said. "That's something that's been missing from *your* life for a while."

Rachel ignored the dig. "I can't let myself get distracted by my personal desires," she said. "This is serious business. If I can prove my man-taming principles work on a he-man like Garret Kelly, I can have a whole new career in television."

"That's a big *if*." Moira added pepper to her salad. "A man who goes by the nickname 'Wild Man' might not respond well to taming."

"I'm not going to fail." *No matter what Denton or Rhonda or anyone else thinks.* "I'm going to devote all my energy to this project. I *will* have that television show."

"I guess there's nothing that says you can't enjoy yourself while you're at it," Moira said. "After all, Garret Kelly is awfully sexy. If you like the big, brawny type."

The memory of Garret's mouth wrapped around her fingers made Rachel squirm in her seat. "Yeah. He's all right."

"*All right?* Girl, you should have seen the women drooling over him at Denton's party. And he asked about you."

She blinked. "He did? What did he say?"

"I mentioned that I was your friend and he said you were very interesting. But he said it in a way that meant he was *interested* in getting to know you better."

"Well, that's good. It should make my job easier." If she could keep from getting distracted by her own rampant lust.

"So, are you just going to walk up to him and

announce that you're the Man Tamer, here to transform him?" Moira asked.

She shook her head. "No. Denton's decided pairing the two of us will make a great publicity stunt. The Wild Man and the Man Tamer—get it? Part of his plan to gain as much press as possible for the Dallas Devils and his new star player."

Getting Garret to go along with the scheme might be a little tricky, but if anyone could do it, Denton could. The man was a master manipulator. He'd play up the publicity angle and Rachel would pretend to go along. If Garret was like most men, he'd have no clue she was working to tame him. It was part of the beauty of her techniques and one reason they were so successful.

She took a bite of salad and chewed thoughtfully, then, anxious to move the conversation away from her impending transformation of Wild Man to Perfect Boyfriend, she asked, "How are things with you and Dave?"

Moira slumped in her chair. "The man is addicted to hockey, basketball and now lacrosse. There's some game on almost every night, and of course he *has* to watch them all. I'd get more attention from him if I painted my body like a scoreboard."

"Hmm. Maybe he's taking for granted you'll always be there. Have you tried ignoring him? Purposely staying away?"

"Would that be 'withholding affection'?" Moira asked.

"Exactly."

"I'm afraid he wouldn't even notice. And where would that leave me?"

Better off? Rachel thought, but she didn't say it.

"Then do you love him enough to resign yourself to being a sports widow?"

"Yes. No. I don't know." Moira fiddled with her fork. "I do love him. And I think deep down, he still loves me. But I don't want to spend the rest of my life being taken for granted this way."

"Then maybe it's time to punish his bad behavior," Rachel said.

"How do I do that? Disconnect his cable?"

Rachel smiled. "That's one alternative. But I was thinking of bringing another man into the picture. Make Dave jealous."

Moira's eyes widened. "I couldn't do that."

"Why not? If Dave's deserted you for professional sports, you can give him a taste of his own medicine by paying attention to someone else."

"Right." Moira looked around. "And where are all these men vying for my attention?"

"They're out there. You haven't noticed them because you're giving off 'taken' vibes. You just have to make yourself available and someone will show up."

"Spoken by someone who hasn't had a steady boyfriend in two years."

"It's only been a little over a year. And I didn't have trouble getting dates before my column became so high profile." At least, Rachel hoped that was the reason. She hated to think men avoided her because of something in her personality.

"Speaking of high profile, did you know your sister's on the front page of the Lifestyles section of today's *Morning News?*"

"What is it this time?" Rachel said. "The Children's Hospital fund-raiser or the Junior League tea?"

"She's the hostess with the mostest for the Winter Fantasy Costume Ball. Apparently it's a big honor."

"And so much more socially acceptable than a tacky daytime television show or bestselling magazine column." Rachel wrinkled her nose. "Well, whoopee for her. I'll have to call and congratulate her."

"Don't let her get to you, Rach." Moira stabbed at her salad. "You know you wouldn't trade places with her for anything. I can't imagine anything more boring than spending your days in meetings and planning sessions with a bunch of other society matrons."

"The money she has would be nice, but you're right—I wouldn't trade places with her."

"I wouldn't be surprised if she doesn't envy you," Moira said.

Rachel laughed. "Oh, you're wrong there. Rhonda is exactly where she always wanted to be. Why would she envy me?"

"Maybe because you're younger, cooler and free to do pretty much anything you want—including date hot guys like Garret Kelly."

Rhonda, envious? The idea was absurd but cheering. "I guess I do have it pretty good," Rachel said. "Not that Garret and I are dating." *Yet.*

"But you are going to be seeing a lot of him," Moira pointed out. "I take it the two of you are supposed to make public appearances and stuff?"

"Something like that." Rachel poked at her salad, searching for a chunk of avocado, a shred of cheese or a candied walnut—something besides greens. "Apparently, Garret's contract obligates him to do publicity for the team, and I'm just going along for the ride."

"Except you have an ulterior motive."

She nodded. "Except for that. But Garret doesn't have to know that. It will probably make it easier on me if he doesn't. Then he won't be trying so hard to resist my techniques."

"What about you? Are you going to resist his techniques?" Moira laughed. "I'm thinking you shouldn't try too hard."

"Very funny." There was no denying the sparks that had passed between her and the hunky athlete at Denton's party. Who was to say she shouldn't use that attraction to her advantage? This was serious business, but no one said she couldn't have fun in the process.

GARRET WAS JUST getting off work Tuesday when his phone rang. "Hullo, mate," he said as he flipped open the phone.

"Is this Wild Man Kelly?" a feminine voice teased.

"The one and only," he said, playing the hale-and-hearty chap despite his wariness that some fan had got hold of his private number.

"This is Rachel Westover. We met at Denton Morrison's party?"

He grinned, uneasiness fleeing. "As if I'd ever forget. Need help with any more chocolate?"

"Um, no. But I was hoping to get together soon."

The knowledge that she'd remembered him, and sought him out, pleased him no end. "How about tonight? I'm just getting off work, so I'll need to clean up a bit, but I could meet you at say—" he checked his watch "—six-thirty?"

"Work? Do you mean, practice?"

"No, I mean a real job. Lacrosse players don't pull in the ready like American football players and such. We have to work for a living like regular blokes."

"So what do you do?"

"I have my own fire and safety company. We install alarm systems, fire extinguishers, that sort of thing in homes and businesses."

"Who knew? So do you want to meet for drinks at six-thirty? There's a club on Fifteenth Street. Tangerine. Do you know it?"

"I can find it. I'll see you there."

On the drive to his apartment, Garret thought about Rachel. He knew very little about her beyond her name and that she worked for Denton in some capacity. And that she had amazingly soft skin and a passion for chocolate. Not a bad foundation for a new relationship, he supposed.

He'd heard no more from Denton about whatever publicity stunt he'd been hatching for him and Rachel. Maybe the team owner had had second thoughts about the Wild Man having a girlfriend.

Garret's contract obligated him to do whatever Denton came up with to promote the team, from making commercials to escorting beautiful models to high-profile events. But what he did on his own time was his business. Rachel Westover was a woman he'd just as soon keep all to himself.

He turned into the lot of his apartment complex, an upscale place owned by Morrison Enterprises. As he was climbing out of his car, Bud Mayhew waved at him from two spaces down. Mayhew was another newcomer to Dallas, as was most of the team. He hailed from Alberta, Canada, and was a pretty quiet guy, letting his skills on the court speak for him.

"Want to come up later and watch the hockey game?" Bud asked, loping over to join Garret.

"Can't, I've got a date."

"Oh? Who with?"

"Lady named Rachel. Met her at Denton's party."

Bud grinned. "Moira's friend, right?"

"That's the one."

"If she's half as good-looking as Moira, you're a lucky man."

Garret glanced at his friend. This was the first time he could remember Bud commenting on a woman. "So you thought Moira was a beauty?" Personally, he didn't go for the skinny, small type. They looked too fragile for a big guy like him to have anything to do with.

"Sure. She was great. And taken." Bud frowned. "Though that Dave guy she was with was a real ass."

"I could get her number from Rachel. You could call her up."

"No thanks." Bud took a step back, shaking his head.

"Why not, mate? It's just a phone call."

Bud shoved his hands into his pockets and stared at the ground. "What would I say? I'd sound like an idiot."

Garret grinned. "We're all idiots, mate. Especially

when it comes to women. Accept that and you'll be a lot better off."

"Yeah, well, I'm not interested in proving it every time I open my mouth." He took another step back. "Go get ready for your date. See ya around."

"See ya." Garret waved at Bud, then took the steps to his apartment two at a time. He could have told Bud that he himself was once the shy, retiring type who had learned to overcome his reticence and get the girl. Of course it would all be ballocks. Garret never found it difficult to talk to people, men or women. The only advice he had for Bud was to get over himself and just do it.

In the past it had been pointed out to him that this wasn't particularly helpful, so that was the end of his advice giving. And he wasn't much for taking advice, either.

After all, no one needed to tell him that he and Rachel had started something at Denton's party. With any luck tonight, they'd keep things going in a very good way.

RACHEL STEPPED INTO Tangerine and let her eyes adjust to the light. There was a good crowd for a Tuesday night, and a DJ was spinning dance tunes from a booth overlooking the smallish dance floor. She spotted Garret at a tall table near the bar and made her way through the crush to him. "Sorry I'm late," she said. "I had trouble finding a parking spot."

"No worries. I haven't been here long." He signaled the waitress. "What can I get you?"

"Diet Coke with lime." She settled into her chair. "I don't like to drink and drive." Not to mention she wanted to keep all her wits about her when dealing with him.

"Smart woman. I took light rail so I'm free to get blotto."

It took half a second for her to realize he was joking. That crooked-tooth grin of his did serious things to her insides. *Get a grip,* she reminded herself, and looked out over the dance floor. She told herself she needed to evaluate him objectively before she began the actual work of applying her man-taming principles.

She studied him out of the corner of her eye. He was wearing a striped button-down shirt, tails untucked, over a dark green T-shirt. He *had* shaved. For her? A good sign.

All in all, she decided her initial impression of him was accurate: good-looking, casual attitude toward dress and grooming, masculine and self-confident. And sexy. She couldn't forget sexy.

His grin transformed into a knowing smile and he winked. "Caught you looking," he said.

She couldn't stop the hot flush that engulfed her face. The curse of being fair-skinned, she told herself.

Her drink arrived and she took a long sip, trying to rein in her libido. She had a job to do here. Garret obviously had rough edges that needed smoothing and she was just the woman to do it. Contrary to what Denton thought, the object was not to emasculate the man, only to bring his behavior up to a higher level.

"You look great," he said. "I'm really glad you called me. I've been meaning to ask Denton for your number."

Did this mean he didn't know about Denton's plans for them? "Has Denton talked to you about me?" she asked.

"No." His smile faded. "Is there something I should know about you and Denton?"

"No! I mean, I'm a writer for a magazine he owns. *Belinda* magazine?"

"Never heard of it. But then, I don't pay much attention to that sort of thing."

Now she was certain Denton hadn't mentioned his scheme to play the "Wild Man meets the Man Tamer" card in the press. And she wasn't going to be the one to tell Garret. With luck, Denton would forget the publicity angle, though she fully intended to hold him to the terms of their bet. Better change the subject. "Tell me about Australia," she said. "How long have you been in the States?"

"A couple of years. I got to know a lot of Yanks when I was doing a tour in Iraq and they convinced me this was the place to be for lacrosse. I played on a good team in Queensland and was able to land a roster spot with the Denver Mammoth. Then Dallas was awarded an expansion team this year and Denton recruited me for that."

The strains of Vivaldi coming from her purse made her jump. She grabbed for the bag. "Sorry, it's my phone."

"Of course." He made a face but said nothing more.

She flipped open the phone and checked the number. Rhonda. What was she doing calling this time of evening?

Rachel shut off the phone and stuffed it back into her bag. "It was my sister. I'll call her back later." She shifted in her chair and returned her focus to their previous conversation. "You were in Iraq?" she asked. "As a soldier?"

"No, I was there as a tourist."

She made a face. "Very funny." Maybe the war wasn't a good topic for casual conversation. "Why lacrosse? Why not basketball or rugby or something else?"

He shrugged. "I played rugby in school, but lacrosse was what I was good at." His grin returned. "It's a sport that requires you to be very good with your hands."

"And you're good with your hands."

"That I am." He took a long drink, eyes locked to hers.

If she didn't know better, she'd have sworn her drink was spiked. How else to explain the tingling in her nerve endings and the flush of heat through her body?

She pushed back her chair. "Let's dance."

He shook his head. "No thanks. I don't dance."

"Everyone dances." She grabbed his hand and tugged. It was like trying to move a boulder. "Come on," she said. "I thought athletes were supposed to be light on their feet."

"Not this one." But he let her pull him out of his chair and lead him toward the dance floor. "Don't come crying to me when your toes are all black and blue."

"Oh please. There are no steps to this kind of dancing. Just move with the music."

Two minutes later she was doing her best not to laugh. But she didn't hide it well enough.

"Don't think I don't see that smirk," he said. He waved his arms in the air like a man trying to flag down a plane. "I told you I wasn't any good at this."

"You're terrible!" she said, bending double with

laughter. She had never met anyone with such a lack of rhythm. "I hope you play lacrosse better than you dance."

"Come to a game and see me. The first one is next week. We're playing the Calgary Roughnecks."

"Maybe I will come." She knew as much about lacrosse as she did bocci ball, but she was willing to make certain sacrifices for the sake of her career.

The music switched abruptly to a slow, dreamy jazz riff. Garret stopped flailing about. "This is more like it," he said.

The next thing she knew, he was pulling her into his arms. His chest was a hard, warm wall she was pressed against, his arms wrapped securely around her. She told herself she should pull back, put some distance between them. Things were happening too quickly and she needed to think.

But being close to him like this felt better than a full-body massage. Not to mention he was a much better dancer at this speed. They swayed together in a gentle rhythm that made her think of other moves they might make, more intimate rhythms they might respond to.

His hand slid down to the base of her spine. The heat of his touch radiated straight to her groin. She squirmed, letting him know he should back off, but that only succeeded in grinding her pelvis against the hard ridge of his erection. She looked up and his eyes met hers. "See what you do to me?" he said.

"You should keep your hands to yourself," she said.

"Sorry. I can't seem to help myself. It's getting to be a habit where you're concerned."

One habit she wasn't sure she wanted him to break. "Have you been drinking champagne again?" she teased.

"No, I'm intoxicated by you."

It was a terrible line, but delivered in heated tones, in that sexy voice of his, it made her melt. This wasn't going at all as she'd imagined.

He bent closer, his mouth very near hers. She shut her eyes and held her breath, anticipating his kiss. She was dying to know what his mouth would feel like. She *needed* to know.

Instead he pushed her away. She opened her eyes and sighed out her breath in exasperation. And men claimed women liked to tease!

"Song's over," he said. But his gaze remained fixed on hers, his eyes dark, intense.

She whirled and started blindly across the floor, intending to find the ladies' room. She needed to get hold of herself. After all, she was the Man Tamer. She was the one who was supposed to be in charge here!

3

Man-Taming Sex
Dear Man Tamer:
There's a really hot guy at work that I'm very attracted to. I think he feels the same way about me. I want to ask him out for drinks but I'm afraid where we might end up. Is it ever okay to have sex on the first date?
Hot to Trot

Dear Hot to Trot:
Will you respect yourself in the morning? If you're secure in yourself, and don't try to delude yourself into thinking it's love at this early stage of the game, I say there's nothing wrong with going for it. If he's as interested as you say, you could have a great time. Just go in with your eyes open, accepting that he may not call you in the morning. And remember to be safe. Bring condoms in case he doesn't.
The Man Tamer

SINCE A COLD SHOWER wasn't readily available, Garret decided he needed a drink. He elbowed his way to the bar and ordered Irish whiskey. Though it would take more than one drink to put out the fire Rachel had started in him.

She returned from the ladies' room, hair freshly combed, lipstick bright on those lips he'd come dangerously close to kissing. Except he'd been afraid he wouldn't be able to stop at one kiss, that he'd have ended up embarrassing them both in front of a dance floor full of people.

"What should we do now?" she asked.

His eyes met hers, trying to read her thoughts. But she was doing that thing women do, looking up at him through her lashes, pulling a lacy veil over her thoughts. "You really want to know what I want to do?" he asked.

She blinked. "Of course."

He set the empty glass on the bar and turned to face her. "I want to take you back to my place and take off all our clothes."

Her lips parted, though she didn't make a sound. A rosy flush washed over her cheeks and her eyes darkened. He'd caught her off guard, but he knew an aroused woman when he saw one. The knowledge made him even hotter.

"I know what you're going to say," he said. "You're not that kind of girl. But you are a woman, and the idea turns you on, doesn't it? Admit it."

She shook her head. "I'm not admitting anything."

Which, to his way of thinking, was as good as a yes. "All right then. Why don't we go someplace quieter and have some coffee. And talk." Talking wasn't as good as taking their clothes off, but it could be its own kind of foreplay.

There was a coffee shop around the corner and over coffee drinks that cost as much as his whiskey they talked about their families. A nice, safe, first-date conversation. He learned she was the youngest of four children, the second girl, with two brothers sandwiched between her and her older sister. Her parents lived in Houston and her siblings were scattered around the state. He told her about his mum, who'd raised him and his three sisters on a factory worker's wages.

"She sounds like an amazing woman," Rachel said.

He nodded. "She is. But after growing up with all that estrogen, it was nice to get out on my own."

"Maybe that's what really attracted you to lacrosse—that it's such a macho game."

"Is that what you think? Then you definitely should come to our first game."

"I wouldn't have any idea what was going on. I don't know anything about the game."

"If you're going to be hanging out with me, it's time you learned."

"And am I going to be hanging out with you?"

Their eyes met and he felt again the rush of blood straight south. "I don't think there's any doubt about that, do you?"

She looked away, but a slow smile formed on her lips. "Are you sure you're up for it?"

"Oh yeah." This might be one time when he really lived up to his nickname "Wild Man."

RACHEL WAITED until the next day to return Rhonda's call. She drummed her nails on the smooth surface of her desk and counted the rings while she waited for her sister to answer. Four…five… "Hello?"

"Finally. What took you so long?"

"I was driving and I had to find a place to pull over," Rhonda said.

Heaven forbid big sister live dangerously. "That's what headsets are for," Rachel said.

"Tell that to all those headset-wearing people with banged-up cars. But I know you didn't call me to argue about cell phones and driving. What's up?"

"You called me," Rachel said. "Last night?"

"Oh, yes. Why didn't you answer then? What were you doing?"

Engaging in what amounted to verbal foreplay with a very sexy man, Rachel thought. She ought to say just that and shock her big sister, but then Rhonda would probably feel compelled to lecture her on safe sex or the evils of promiscuity or something. Not that Rachel was promiscuous, but she didn't feel like debating the point with Rhonda. "I was busy," she said. "What do you want?"

"I want to know if you've abandoned this crazy idea of going on television with this whole man-taming thing."

Of course. Rhonda lived in fear that one of her society friends would learn she was related to the woman who wrote the Man Taming column for *Belinda* magazine. All that talk about sex—so tacky, don't you know? "Why would I abandon the idea?" Rachel said. "It's a great idea and it's going to be very successful."

"You could be successful in so many other ways," Rhonda said. "You don't have to stoop to this."

Of course Rhonda saw all this talk about sex as beneath her or her sister. Rachel bit back an angry retort and decided to take a different approach—one that relied on one of her own positive reinforcement principles. "I saw the article about the Winter Fantasy ball," she said. "Congratulations."

As Rachel had hoped, her words threw Rhonda off balance. There was a long silence, then Rhonda cleared her throat. "Thank you," she said. "I was really honored to be named official hostess."

Rachel resisted the urge to laugh. After all the money Harrison had donated to the effort, if Rhonda hadn't been named hostess, heads would have rolled. "I'm sure you'll do a great job," she said.

"Why are you being so nice to me all of a sudden?" Rhonda asked.

Rachel did laugh this time. "What do you mean? You're my sister. Can't I be nice to my sister?"

"I get it. You're just trying to make it up to me for embarrassing me all these months with that column of yours."

"If you're embarrassed, that's your problem, not mine," Rachel said coolly. "I'm very proud of my work."

"Oh please. Man taming?" Rhonda lowered her voice. "It sounds so…so slutty."

Rachel laughed again. "Obviously you've never read my column or you'd know that it has nothing to do with sex. In fact, maybe you ought to read it. You might learn something that would help your marriage."

"My marriage is just fine, thank you very much." Rhonda's voice was clipped, conveying her deep offense. Then she responded with a classic Rhonda retort. "At least I have a husband."

"Never mind that," Rachel snapped. "I'm sorry if it embarrasses you. You'll just have to find a way to get over that."

"I'm not thinking of me right now," Rhonda said. "I'm thinking of you. No man in his right mind is going to want to be seen anywhere near a woman known as the Man Tamer. You might as well check yourself into a convent this minute."

"A real man wouldn't be threatened by the idea." She tried not to sound defensive, but Rhonda must have heard something in her voice anyway.

"Tell me how many dates you've had since that column of yours started running?" Rhonda asked.

Rachel smiled. "I had a date just last night," she said.

"Who with?"

"None of your business. I'm seeing him again on Friday."

"You'd better tell me who it is."

"Why should I?"

"If you don't, I'll tell Mom about the time you spent the weekend with that guitarist when you told her you were at the beach with friends."

"That was five years ago."

"You think Mom won't care? She was a virgin when she married Dad, you know." A fact both girls had heard often in their teen years, much to their deep embarrassment.

"I know." Rachel hesitated, imagining the lectures she'd have to endure from their mother, who still clung to the fantasy that a woman who had remained single in her late twenties was as pure as a preadolescent milk-maid. "All right, it's Garret Kelly."

"Who?" Rhonda was no doubt searching her mental database of socially prominent eligible bachelors and coming up blank. Which meant her sister was dating a nobody. The horror!

Rachel's smile broadened. "Garret Kelly. Star of the Dallas Devils lacrosse team."

"Oh. An athlete." Worse than a nobody to Rhonda's way of thinking.

"Hey, he's a great guy and a lot of fun."

"Just what I want in a serious relationship," Rhonda said dryly. "You're almost thirty. You can't play the party girl forever."

"I will if it will keep me from acting like someone who sucks lemons for fun," Rachel said. "Listen, this has been a ball, but I've got work to do. Goodbye."

Before Rhonda could say anything else, Rachel hung up, then sat back and stared at the phone. The two sisters knew just what to say to push each other's buttons, so that almost every conversation became a verbal duel.

Usually, Rachel enjoyed sparring with Rhonda. Big sister was so predictable. It was fun to poke holes in Rhonda's inflated sense of propriety.

But today she found little joy in the aftermath of this conversation. She'd secretly hoped that by acknowledging the importance to Rhonda of chairing the Winter Fantasy ball that her sister might extend a similar olive branch and be happy—for once—that Rachel's career was going great and that she was about to realize her dream of her own television show.

If not that, then couldn't Rhonda have been more excited about Rachel's date with Garret Kelly? Couldn't they have laughed and shared confidences, the way sisters were supposed to do?

She sighed and opened a new file on her computer. Rhonda was Rhonda and there was no sense trying to change her. And she'd never stop trying to change Rachel, but that was a losing battle. Rhonda would never realize that Rachel didn't want to be respectable and modest. Not when the alternative was so much more fun.

RACHEL CONVINCED MOIRA to come with her to the Dallas Devils game Friday night. "Tell me again why we're doing this," Moira said when she met Rachel at the light-rail station. "You hate sports. So do I, for that matter."

"But you're my best friend so you'll come to support me, right?" Rachel fed dollar bills into the ticket machine. The train would drop them right at the stadium, saving the huge hassle of parking downtown.

"You don't need my support." Moira accepted her ticket. "Though you must have it really bad for Garret Kelly if you let him talk you into coming to a game."

"I'm doing this for my career, remember," Rachel said. Well, mostly for her career. Seeing Garret again was merely a bonus.

"Oh, right. The bet. What does the Wild Man think about that?"

"He doesn't know. Denton didn't tell him and I'm certainly not going to." The train arrived and they climbed aboard.

Moira plopped into the seat beside Rachel and shook her head. "I don't know. What's going to happen when he finds out?"

"*If* he finds out, I'll laugh it off as another of Denton's publicity stunts. He's always coming up with crazy stuff like that."

"Then why not tell Garret now and get it over with?"

"Because…" She chewed her lower lip. "Because I really like Garret and I don't want him flipping out over the whole Man Tamer thing."

"He's going to find out about your column one of these days. Especially if you take it to TV."

"But by then he'll know me better. Plus, I'll have applied my principles to our relationship and he'll see how great they've been for both of us."

"I'll believe that when I see it."

"I know you haven't had much success with David," Rachel said. "But I think that's because you haven't given my approach time to take effect." Granted, maybe the man-taming principles didn't work for everyone. But letters from her readers and her own studies into behavior modification assured her they were effective most of the time.

"One thing I don't understand is, I thought your techniques were designed for women to use on their boyfriends or husbands. You and Garret hardly know each other."

"Yes, but that could change."

"Oh?" Moira leaned toward her, her expression avid. "So I was right when I said he was interested in you, too."

"You could say that. He asked me to go to bed with him last night."

Moira laughed. "If every man who wanted to have sex with you qualified as a boyfriend, you wouldn't have a free night in the week."

"Maybe, but this was different." Rachel allowed herself a small smile. "I wanted to go to bed with him, too."

"Then why didn't you?"

She sat up straighter. "We'd just met!"

Moira shrugged. "What better way to really get to know a man?"

She had a point, Rachel conceded. The train arrived at their station and they were swept along in the crowd making its way to the arena. They found their seats—center court, front row, thanks to Garret—and settled in. "Looks like a hockey setup without the ice." Moira pointed to the nets at each end of the court. "Those are the same as hockey, too."

"How do you know so much?" Rachel asked.

"I guess I picked up a few things from David."

Just then the arena went dark and an announcer's voice boomed. "Get ready to welcome your Dallas Devils!" With an explosion of fireworks and the blare of heavy-metal music, a double line of motorcycles raced into the arena. On the back of each was perched a scantily clad dancer. Behind them, heralded by more fireworks, the players, clad in shorts, loose jerseys, gloves and helmets, raced in.

The crowd screamed and whistled, louder even than

the music. Rachel wanted to clamp her hands over her ears, but refrained. "There's Garret!"

Moira pointed to the fourth man in the first row of players—number thirty-six, the name Kelly stitched across the back. Rachel probably wouldn't have recognized him. The helmet covered his head and the padded jersey made his shoulders even broader. Her gaze shifted to the only part of him that wasn't covered. "Nice legs," she said. They were muscular and toned, dusted with brown hair.

"They all have nice legs," Moira said appreciatively. "Too bad the shorts aren't tighter, though."

After the Canadian and American anthems were played, they settled in to watch the game. Rachel's bottom had barely touched the seat before the crowd roared and surged to its feet again. "Devils' goal!" the announcer shouted. Lights flashed and music pounded as the players raced to the end of the court.

"What happened?" Rachel asked.

"We scored, I guess."

The rest of the game was like that. The action shifted from one end of the court to the other with lightning speed. The Devils scored another goal, then the Roughnecks came back to score three. Thank God for replays or Rachel never would have figured out what was happening.

Even then, she found it impossible to see how anyone could catch a hard rubber ball in a small net at the end of a stick, then run the length of the court with it, all while opposing players whacked at him with their sticks. And then the player with the ball somehow had to fire it past a giant man in pads who stood in front of the net and tried to block the shot. Yet it happened over and over again, on both sides.

In the middle of the second quarter, Garret was sentenced to two minutes in the penalty box. Rachel had no idea why, but the crowd alternately jeered and cheered when the penalty was announced. They cheered again when Garret rejoined the action on the court.

In fact, they spent most of the time cheering. Or waving signs. Or singing along with the loud rock music that blared during every time-out. Rachel had never seen such a rowdy crowd. "These people are scary," she told Moira. "It's like a religious revival or something."

"I think it's kind of fun," Moira said. "I might even ask David to take me to a game. This is a lot more exciting than baseball."

A little more than two hours after it began, the game ended with the score Devils 17, Roughnecks 16. The crowd went wild, then dispersed rapidly. Moira and Rachel stayed courtside to greet Garret.

He spotted them and came over. He'd removed his helmet and his hair, damp with sweat, looked darker than before. The stubble was back along his jaw and his jersey was torn at the neck. But he was smiling, teeth flashing. "Was that a great game or what?" he asked.

"It was great," Moira said.

"Things certainly happen fast in lacrosse," Rachel said.

"Never a dull moment. Hey, thanks a lot for coming out."

"Thanks for getting us the great tickets." She nodded

to the stick in his hand. On one end was an elaborately woven net. "What do they call that stick?" she asked.

"A stick." He laughed. "How's that for fancy lingo?"

"Great game, Garret!" Another player, shorter with blond hair, skidded up to them. He grinned at the women. "Can you believe this man? Five goals and three assists."

"Bud Mayhew," Garret said. "Bud, you remember Moira. And this is Rachel."

"Hey." Bud nodded to them, but said nothing further.

"I remember you," Moira said. "You were at Denton's party."

"Yeah." He looked around nervously. "Hey, I better get to the locker room. See you around." He turned and hurried away.

Moira frowned after him. "Not very friendly, is he?"

"Aw, Bud's a great guy. He's just shy around women."

"I don't know why he would be. He's cute." Moira grinned. "Nice legs."

"I'll tell him you said so." Garret turned to Rachel. "Let me get cleaned up and I'll take you two out to celebrate."

"I can't. I have to get home," Moira said. She patted Rachel's shoulder. "But you stay."

Rachel wanted to tell Moira she didn't have to go out of her way to leave the two of them alone. Part of the reason she'd asked her friend here tonight was to slow things down with Garret. Of course, after their conversation on the train, she was questioning why she should even bother. After all, she and Garret were both single adults. If the attraction between them was so strong, why *not* act on it?

When Garret returned from the locker room he wore a blue sport coat, tan slacks and a white shirt open at the throat. He'd shaved and he smelled of expensive cologne. Rachel nodded approvingly. "You clean up pretty well."

"I try." He ushered her out of the arena, one hand at the small of her back.

"Where are we going?" she asked.

"I hear O'Malley's has good steaks." He punched his key chain and a black supercab Titan pickup winked its headlights at them. Rachel almost laughed. Of course he drove a truck. This was Texas and real men drove big trucks.

He opened the door for her—give him points for manners—and she slid into the leather seat. When he started the engine, rap music blasted from the stereo. He leaned over and stabbed it off. "Sorry about that," he said.

"Please tell me you don't rap along with the radio," she said.

He grinned. "Only when I'm alone."

At O'Malley's they were ushered to a corner table. They ordered drinks and Garret studied her across the table. "Tell me what you thought of the game," he said.

"It was exciting, but everything happened so fast I still don't have any idea what was going on. Obviously, the object is to shoot the ball into the opposing team's net, but I could never keep track of where the ball was. Or how anyone managed to get it past the goalie."

"That's the beauty of the game." He leaned toward

her, elbows on the table, and arranged salt and pepper shakers, condiment bottles and glasses onto a "court" defined by their silverware. "Let's say I get the ball. If I have a lot of defenders on me, I'm going to pass it to a teammate who's open. If I'm open, I run down the court, cradling the ball in my stick. I'll either pass it again to an open man or, if I see an opening, I'll fire it into the net. I may have to shoot low or high to get past the goalie. My teammates try to block so he can't see it coming."

"Slow down. What's cradling the ball?"

"Rocking it back and forth in the pocket of my stick. Like a baby. Think of it like dribbling in basketball. You're not allowed to just hold the ball."

She shook her head. "I still don't see how anyone ever makes a goal."

"Practice and skill." He sipped his drink. "I told you, I'm very good with my stick." He winked, a slow opening and closing of one eye that made her catch her breath and want to fan herself.

I'll just bet you are, she thought.

The waiter arrived to take their order, then Garret picked up the conversation again. "Now you know all about what I do for a living. Tell me more about your writing. What do you write?"

She hesitated. "I told you I write for a magazine called *Belinda.* For women."

"But what do you write? Fashion tips? Investigative reporting? Gossip column?"

She could have found a way to blow him off, or lie, but she really wasn't "that kind of girl." She took a long drink of wine, then squared her shoulders and said, "I write a column called 'The Man Tamer.' I give advice to women on how to deal with their boyfriends or husbands."

"'The Man Tamer'?" Garret choked on his drink. "Crikey, that's rich. You're serious?"

She nodded. "It's a very popular column. Probably the most popular feature in the magazine."

He wiped his mouth on a napkin and sat back, studying her. "And what qualifies you to know how to tame a man?"

"I have a degree in behavioral psychology from Southern Methodist University."

"But have you had a lot of experience with men?"

The seriousness of his voice and the intensity of his gaze implied much more than the simple words of his question. "If you're asking, am I a slut, the answer is no." She raised her chin. "I'm pretty particular about who I date."

"You must not be too picky, since you agreed to go out with me."

"Maybe the Man Tamer thinks the Wild Man would be an interesting challenge," she said.

Did she imagine the spark of interest in his eyes? He said nothing as their meals were set in front of them. He attacked his steak with gusto. Watching a man devour food was not normally high on Rachel's list of preferred activities, but she had to admit, there was something about the *passion* with which Garret ate that did funny things to her insides.

The atmosphere of the entire meal was charged, her senses heightened. The food tasted better, the wine was sweeter and she was keenly aware of the man across from her—the scent of his aftershave, the warmth of his leg when it brushed hers, the heat of his gaze on her.

He paid the check and, in silence, they walked to his truck. He stopped before opening the passenger door and turned her to face him. "There's something I've been wanting to do for a while now," he said. Then he kissed her.

There was nothing tentative or hesitant about this kiss. His lips covered hers, staking a claim, sending a rush of feeling through her. Garret kissed the same way he played lacrosse or ate a steak—with his whole focus and great skill. His tongue teased her, sending molten currents through every limb. One hand caressed her shoulder, gently kneading, while the other hand braced against the trunk. She was caught between the cool metal and the hard heat of his body yet she could think of no place she would rather be at the moment.

She was breathless and light-headed—and very aroused—when he finally broke away. The devilish light in his eyes made her legs even more wobbly. "I should warn you," he said. "Winning makes me horny."

She managed a shaky laugh. "I have a feeling breathing makes you horny," she said.

"Only around you." He inhaled deeply. "I like your perfume."

"I'm not wearing perfume."

"Even better." He opened the door and touched her elbow. "Want to come back to my place? Just for coffee."

That hadn't been a *just for coffee* kiss but she let it

slide. Better to go with the flow tonight. "I'd love that." Even if they really only had coffee, she wanted to see his place. You could tell a lot about a man from his apartment.

4

Is Man Taming Right for You?
Dear Man Tamer:
I've been reading your column for a while now and really love it. After a lot of years of dating, I've finally found the man I think is The One! He has a few rough edges that I don't really mind, but I'm wondering if after we're married these few bad habits will really annoy me. Should I employ your man-taming principles now to head off trouble later?
Hoping for Happily-ever-after

Dear Hoping:
I believe it's never too early to put my principles into effect. And the easiest time by far to use them is when you're still in the honeymoon phase of a relationship, when his desire to please you is strongest. So get to work and insure a happy future for both of you.
The Man Tamer

GARRET SPENT THE DRIVE to his apartment telling himself to calm down. To slow down. Rachel was a classy lady and he didn't want to blow it with her before things even got started. They'd have coffee. Just coffee.

Who was he kidding? His one goal in life right now was to convince her to take her clothes off. She thought she knew a lot about men—he'd show her one who was anything but tame.

Barking greeted them as he inserted his key in the lock. Rachel's eyes widened. "What is that?"

"That's Barney. Don't worry about him. He's a big goof." He shoved open the door and Barney bounded to greet them, a whirlwind of brown fur and flopping ears and wagging tail. Garret managed to insert himself between Rachel and the dog, saving her from the worst of the drool. "Down, fella!" he shouted. "Sit! Sit!"

Considering the dog had flunked obedience training, it wasn't a big surprise that Barney ignored the command. Instead he flopped over onto his back, tongue lolling, tail thwacking the sofa. "That's a good boy," Garret enthused. He rubbed the dog's tummy and Barney's eyes half closed in bliss.

"He certainly is…big," Rachel said, eyeing the canine warily. "What kind is he?"

"He's a bitzer."

"A bitzer? I've never heard of that breed."

"It means he's a bit of this and a bit of that." He collected half a dozen odd items of clothing from the floor and furniture and chucked them into the hall closet, then took off his sport coat and flung it over the back of the sofa. "Make yourself at home. I'll put the coffee on."

When he returned, Rachel was perched on the edge

of a chair, frowning at the dog. Barney was on the sofa, leaning as close to her as he could, panting happily, tail waving wildly. "I think he likes you," Garret said as he dragged the dog off the sofa.

"He's certainly…affectionate."

"Don't worry about him." Garret fished a dog biscuit from his pocket and whistled at Barney. "Here's a treat for you, boy." He launched the biscuit toward the spare bedroom on the opposite side of the apartment. The dog sailed after it. When he was all the way inside the room, Garret got up and closed the door. "He won't bother us now," he said.

He moved to the stereo and riffled through the CDs scattered atop it. He discarded several raucous rap releases and one bawdy comedy, and chose soft blues. Something to set the mood. And maybe to calm things down. Now that he and Rachel were finally alone, he was uncharacteristically nervous. Maybe it was all her talk of man taming, or the fact that he wanted her more than he'd wanted a woman in a long time. He felt like a boy on his first date with the school hottie.

"I'd better check on the coffee," he said, and started toward the kitchen.

"Don't bother." She intercepted him, one hand on his chest, her body moving in close to his. "I don't think either one of us is really interested in coffee, do you?"

Before he could answer, her lips covered his in a searing kiss that made him forget about coffee, or Barney, or anything but the feel of her in his arms. He walked backward in the direction of the bedroom, their arms wrapped around each other, lips still locked. The

thought of the unmade bed and scattered clothes mo-
mentarily distracted him, but then she started tugging
his shirttails out of his trousers and every thought not
directly connected to Rachel and sex fled for the night.

She was fumbling with the buttons of his shirt when
he literally ripped it off and flung it across the room.
His pants quickly followed, along with shorts, shoes and
socks. She watched him, an odd smile playing about her
lips, as if she was trying not to laugh.

"What's so funny?" he asked, glancing down at his
own naked body. The old fellow was standing at attention, so no worries in that department.

She shook her head. "You don't waste any time, do
you?"

"I don't want to waste a second that could be spent
making love to you." He advanced toward her. "And I'm
starting to feel lonely, the only one in the room without
my clothes on."

"Then I'd better join you." But she took a step back,
refusing to let him touch her. "You watch. I don't want
anything ripping or any buttons popping."

"Your wish is my command." He backed up to the
bed and sat.

She undressed slowly, carefully folding each garment and placing it on a chair behind her. He followed
every movement with his eyes, scarcely daring to blink,
reveling in each new part of her that was revealed. She
had long legs, full breasts and rounded stomach and
hips that begged to be caressed and embraced. His
fingers dug into the bedcovers, anticipating touching
her. He liked that she was willing to undress in front of

him, to admit that she wanted him as much as he wanted her. When she was completely naked, he motioned toward her. "Come here."

She advanced slowly, full breasts swaying slightly with each step, the motion making him dry-mouthed and painfully hard. He thought she would sit beside him, but instead she straddled him and wrapped her arms around him as she delivered another scorching kiss.

He pulled her tight against him, the head of his penis pressed against the soft skin of her belly, the hard points of her breasts cool against his chest. He cupped her bottom with one hand, then traced the smooth line of her thigh. "I've been dreaming about this since I saw you with chocolate dripping off your fingers," he said, his mouth against her neck, breathing in the sweet scent of her.

She flattened her palms against his chest and pushed him back onto the bed. "When you licked that chocolate off my fingers, I thought I'd come right there in the middle of the ballroom," she said.

"I'd like to see you come now." He wriggled up to the top of the bed and she followed after him, until they were lying side by side on the wrinkled sheets.

She raised up on one elbow and studied his face. "You're not afraid of the Man Tamer?" she asked, her tone teasing.

"I wouldn't say fear is anything close to what I'm feeling now." He took her hand and lowered it to his erection. "What I'm feeling now is fairly well crazed with lust for a certain gorgeous blonde."

She squeezed gently, eliciting a groan from deep in

his throat. "Careful there," he cautioned. "That thing's loaded and it might go off."

She released him and lay back beside him, her hand on his chest. "I suppose this is the time for the unromantic talk of our sexual histories, et cetera, et cetera."

"You want to know who I've slept with before?" He turned to look at her. "You don't think that kind of thing is something of a buzz killer?"

She raised up on one elbow and glanced down at his erection. "It doesn't look in danger of dying yet. I don't want specifics, just tell me if there's anything I should worry about."

"No. For one thing, the team physical tested me for every disease known to humankind and pronounced me fit and ready. And for second, I'm not one for shagging any sheila that comes my way."

"That's good to know." She smiled and lay back again.

He waited, but when she remained silent he nudged her. "What about you? Anything I should worry about?"

"Only that I haven't had sex with anyone in going on a year in a half and I'm liable to leave you exhausted. I hope you've got plenty of condoms."

He rolled toward her. "No worries in that department, I promise."

Garret moved quickly from kissing Rachel's lips to kissing her neck, shoulders and breasts. She threaded her fingers through his hair and urged him on as his mouth traced a path across her torso. Nerve endings she'd forgotten existed came alive at his touch. His hands stroked her stomach and hips, fingers circling but never quite coming into contact with her mons. She arched toward him, but he pushed her gently down again and she smiled. She could appreciate a man who didn't want to hurry.

The smile vanished in a rush of indrawn breath as his mouth closed over her breast. His tongue flicked back and forth across the sensitive tip, making her gasp and curl her fingers into the bedcovers. He sucked hard, desire lancing through her and she raked her nails down his back, unable to hold back a moan.

"Like that, did you?" She felt his smile against her skin as he transferred his attention to her other breast. The tension within her built until she felt at the breaking point. When had a man ever brought her to this level of arousal so quickly?

He slid farther down her body, his tongue trailing wet heat around her navel, down her thigh, across the sensitive flesh of her inner thigh. She arched toward him again, silently pleading, and this time he obliged, parting the curls and sweeping his tongue across her clit. She cried out in delight as he began to stroke her, then was silenced again by waves of sensation.

She was dimly conscious of his hands on her hips, pressing her down into the bedcovers, of her fingers kneading his broad shoulders, of his hair tickling her skin.

And then she was aware of nothing but the need building within her, the tension coiling tighter and tighter, her body taut, poised on a single pinpoint of desire.

Release flooded her with warmth and light. She imagined she might have flown from the bed if Garret had not held her so securely. A fanciful idea that no less pleased her, particularly the thought of him as her anchor.

Before she had time to fully return to her senses, he had sheathed himself and entered her. The not unpleasant sensation of long-unused muscles stretching to accommodate him sent a fresh wave of desire through her. She grasped his shoulders and looked into his eyes.

He smiled and stroked her hair. "It feels so good to be in you," he said, then began to move, long, deep strokes that filled her then left her craving more. She thrust her hips up to meet him on each return, and moved her hands down to grasp his buttocks, urging him deeper still.

His eyes lost focus and she closed hers and threw her head back, reveling in the increased tempo he set, feeling his body tense and muscles bunch beneath her hands.

He came with a loud cry and a fierce thrust that made her open her eyes wide. He cradled her head on his shoulder as he moved more gently in her, then, still in her, rolled onto his back, bringing her with him.

For a long moment the only sound was the rasp of their ragged breathing, and the slide of the sheets as he pulled the bedcovers over them. After a while she moved over beside him, her head cradled in his shoulder.

"Amazing," he said. At least that's what she thought he meant. His voice was muffled by the arm he'd thrown over his eyes.

Yeah, pretty amazing, she thought. Because she'd been celibate so long or because she and Garret had essentially been engaging in foreplay for the last week? Or because of something else she couldn't yet define?

This bet with Denton could turn out to be even easier to pull off than she'd imagined. After all, if she and Garret were so compatible in the bedroom, she shouldn't have any trouble at all persuading him to her way of thinking in everything else. Clean up the apartment, incorporate a few grooming tips, do something about that dog…she'd have him tamed in no time.

"I think this is going to work out great," she said. "Don't you?"

The Wild Man's only answer was a snore.

RACHEL WOKE REALIZING she'd made a mistake. She'd allowed personal feelings to get in the way of her goal. Yes, sex with Garret had been awesome and fulfilling and all those things—but was it going to get her her own television show?

It wasn't too late to take charge of the relationship, however. And if she was careful, she wouldn't even have to give up the awesome sex. Time to put her first man-taming principle into action.

By the time Garret woke, Rachel was dressed and making coffee in the kitchen. "Mmm, something smells good." He came up behind her and enveloped her in a hug. "And it's not the coffee. Want to come back to bed?"

She tried to ignore the way even a simple hug from him made her toes curl. "It's tempting, but I thought I'd make breakfast while you shower and shave."

"I thought women liked that stubbly look." He rubbed his chin.

"It *looks* sexy, but it's a little rough on certain, um, tender parts," she said.

"Hmm. If I shave, will you point out exactly which parts?" He pulled her close once more and nuzzled her neck.

Her inner nympho was shouting at her to forget breakfast and take Garret up on his offer, but she forced herself to be strong. She gently pushed him away. "Go on, now. I can't concentrate when you're around."

He leered at her. "You say that like it's a bad thing." But he turned and left the room, whistling off key.

She found eggs and bacon in the refrigerator, though the bacon looked as if it had been there awhile. The bread was stale, too, but maybe once toasted it wouldn't matter. No butter, but she unearthed a jar of marmalade from the back of the fridge. It had an Australian label, so she guessed his mother must have sent it to him.

Once she heard the shower running, she abandoned breakfast preparations and raced into the bedroom and headed for his closet. Jeans, shirts and suits were arranged haphazardly on the rod. She pulled out what looked to be the newest pair of jeans and a semi-stylish shirt and knocked on the bathroom door. No reply, but she thought she heard a very bad rendition of "Take Me to the River" rising up over the rush of running water.

The water stopped and a few seconds later, the door opened. Garret jumped back, obviously startled to see her, but he recovered quickly. "Coming to join me?" he asked, flashing a devilish grin.

Why was she standing here? She'd forgotten as soon as he opened the door and she was confronted with his naked body in all its glory. Water gleamed on well-defined muscles and sparkled in his chest hair. Her gaze fixed on a single drop and followed its path down his body, across washboard abs to the top of his rock-hard thighs, disappearing in the thick thatch of pubic hair. As if responding to her gaze, his penis twitched.

"The old fellow says hello," Garret said.

She blinked, struggling for composure and some coherent thought. "Why do you call it that?" she asked.

"The old fellow?" He shrugged. "Just an Aussie saying." He advanced toward her. "Once you know him better, maybe you can come up with your own pet name."

She stepped back, fending him off with the clothes she still held in one hand. "I love this blue shirt," she said. "It looks so great with your eyes. Will you wear it for me?"

He eyed the shirt. "A little dressy for the weekend, don't you think?"

"What do you usually wear on the weekend?" Not that she didn't already have a good idea. A T-shirt and shorts, she was guessing.

"A T-shirt and shorts." He strode to a dresser and pulled out a shirt and held it up for inspection. A well-endowed young woman hoisted a mug of beer beneath the slogan Make Mine XXXX!

She winced. "Nice, but, uh, there's a hole in it." She pointed to a rip above the woman's left shoulder.

He put his finger through the tear, immediately making it larger. "Ventilation," he said, and grinned.

She held up her choice again. "The blue really brings out your eyes."

He began digging through the dresser once more. "I've got a blue one in here somewhere."

The blue shirt he found advertised a popular brand of beer. "I thought you didn't like American beer," she said.

"Yeah, but the shirt was free. And it's blue."

She held out her choice once more. "I'd really love to see you in this."

He tossed the blue T-shirt aside. "I tell you what. Let's forget about clothes altogether. We'll spend the day in bed. Naked."

He started toward her again, but just then a pitiful wail filled the apartment. Rachel dropped the shirt and looked around for the source of the horrible sound. "Is that a fire alarm or something?"

"It's Barney. I'd say he's ready to come out of the guest room."

She'd forgotten all about Garret's dog. She watched in dismay as he retrieved the blue T-shirt from the floor and put it on, along with a pair of baggy cargo shorts. "I'd better take him for a walk before he ruins the carpet." He kissed her cheek. "I'll be right back."

Rachel returned to the kitchen. Her attempt to influence Garret's wardrobe choices hadn't succeeded as well as she hoped, but the training was only beginning. At least he'd chosen a *blue* shirt. One without holes. That had to be considered something of a victory, right?

WHILE BARNEY SNIFFED trash cans and watered rosebushes, Garret thought about Rachel. She was terrific. She was the one thing that had been lacking in his life since coming to Dallas. Not just the sex, though that was great, but someone to talk to who smelled nice and didn't belch. Plus she was easy to be with. Not always trying to remake a guy like some women. Of course, it was early days, but he had a good feeling about her.

Back at his apartment, Barney was thrilled to see Rachel, too. As soon as Garret unclipped his leash the dog galloped into the kitchen, barking happily. Garret heard a squeal, then a sound like a sack of potatoes falling. He rushed in to see what all the commotion was about.

He found Rachel on her back in the middle of the kitchen, Barney straddling her, covering her face in wet doggy kisses. "Get him away from me!" she said, trying to fend him off with her hands.

"He obviously likes you." Garret grabbed the dog by the collar and pulled him away from her. "Either that, or he smells the bacon you've been cooking. He's very fond of bacon."

He ordered the dog to sit, then helped Rachel to her feet. "Look at me," she said, staring down at her dress. The front was covered with large, muddy dog prints.

"Sorry about that," Garret said. "I'll buy you a new one." Partly to distract her from the dog, and partly because he wanted to hold her again, he took her in his arms. "I don't think we've said a proper good morning."

She didn't resist, and in fact welcomed his kiss, molding her body to his as he pulled her closer. Her lips parted and he tasted the bitter richness of coffee on her tongue. Now this was the way to start a morning.

Barney barked, demanding breakfast. Reluctantly,

Garret released Rachel. "I'd better check on breakfast," she said. Her face was flushed, her hair mussed—he'd never seen a woman look more delectable.

"I'm hungry, but not for food," he said.

She looked away, but not before he saw her smile. "Well, I'm starved. Let's eat."

They turned to find Barney, front paws braced on the counter, nose buried in the plate of bacon. "Barney, no!" Garret shouted.

The dog raised his head, the last strip of bacon dangling from his mouth, and wagged his tail. "Get out of here, you worthless baggage," Garret said, shooing him away.

Rachel laughed. "It's probably just as well," she said. "The bacon looked a little old."

"I'm not surprised," he said, taking a plate from the cabinet and moving to the stove. "I'm not much of a cook. Hey, the eggs and toast look good, though." He filled his plate, then looked at her. "Sorry. You wanted some, too, right?"

She stared. "That's six eggs. And six pieces of toast."

He looked at the food on his plate. It didn't look like so much to him. "I burn a lot of calories running up and down the court during games." He took another plate from the cabinet and transferred half the eggs and toast to it, then handed it to her. "There you go."

She laughed again. Definitely a sound he liked hearing. "I could never eat all that." She took a single piece of toast and couple of spoonfuls of egg. "There. You can have the rest."

They sat at the counter that separated the kitchen from

the dining room to eat their breakfast. He poured fresh coffee, then fetched a jar of Vegemite from the cupboard.

"What is that?" she asked, staring as he spread the black paste on a slice of toast.

"Vegemite." He took a bite and washed it down with coffee. "Aussies are raised on this the way you Yanks are raised on peanut butter."

She picked up the jar and eyed it warily. "Yes, but what is it?"

"Dunno." He took the jar from her and read. "Says here it's yeast extract and flavorings."

She made a face. "I'll stick with marmalade, thank you."

"You don't know what you're missing." He scooped up more scrambled eggs. "Breakfast is good, by the way. Thanks."

"Eggs and toast aren't exactly a challenge," she said.

She dabbed at the corners of her mouth with a napkin. One of those dainty, feminine gestures he found fascinating.

"What are your plans for today?" she asked.

"This morning I'm headed over to a boys and girls club to help with the lacrosse team they've organized there."

"Is that part of your duties as the public face of the team?"

He frowned. "No. It's something I wanted to do. The kids are great."

"Sorry, I shouldn't have said that." She looked down at the table. "My sister is very big on charitable events, but she mostly does it as a way of getting her name and picture in the paper."

"And who's your sister?"

"Rhonda MacMillan? She's married to Harrison MacMillan, the oil tycoon."

He tossed Barney a piece of Vegemite-smeared toast. "Every third person I meet in Texas claims to be an oil tycoon. Can't say I've heard of your sister. Is she as good-looking as you?"

"No, I'm definitely the cuter one."

She winked and he burst out laughing. "You should come with me this morning," He pushed aside his empty plate and drained his coffee cup. "You'd probably get a kick out of it and afterward, you could show me around. I really haven't seen that much of the city. You could show me the sights." Of course the sight he most wanted to see was her naked, back in his bed. What could he say? He had a one-track mind. Not that different from most men he knew, for that matter.

She looked down at her dress. "I'll have to go home and change," she said. "I can't go out like this."

"No worries." He stood. "I'll lend you something of mine."

Her eyes widened. "I can't wear your clothes. For one thing, you're much bigger than I am."

"No, it'll work. You'll see."

She followed him into the bedroom, where he dug through the drawers again and came up with a T-shirt that had shrunk in the wash and a pair of gym shorts that were too tight. "Try these on."

She eyed them as if they might have germs, then shrugged and retreated into the bathroom.

He stuffed the clothes that had fallen onto the floor

during his search back into the dresser and kicked a pair of dirty socks under the bed. He could retrieve them later when he was ready to do the wash.

The bathroom door opened and Rachel emerged, and he whistled. "My clothes never looked so good," he announced.

She'd knotted the shirt at her waist and rolled up the sleeves and the legs of the shorts. The results looked both sexy and hip. "I feel ridiculous," she said.

"You look great." He put his arm around her and steered her toward the door. It was either that, or back to bed, but he had the kids to think about. They'd spend the day getting to know each other better and tonight they could go round two.

She stopped in the doorway. "Aren't you going to make the bed?"

He looked over his shoulder at the tangle of sheets in the middle of the king-size bed. The comforter had slid to the floor and one pillow leaned against the nightstand. "Right." He strode to the bed, tossed the pillow back on, snapped the sheets into place and threw the cover over the whole thing. "That should do it," he said.

He fed Barney a biscuit, made sure the coffeepot was switched off, then led the way to his truck. He took Carpenter Freeway toward downtown Dallas. They passed a billboard with a ten-foot-high image of his face with the legend "Wild Man Kelly And The Dallas Devils—Lacrosse Rocks!

"Nice picture," Rachel said. "Dare I ask how you got the nickname Wild Man?"

"Would you believe me if I told you it was because of my reputation in the bedroom?" He winked.

She bit back a smile and looked out the window. "Did someone kiss and tell or have you been bragging on yourself?"

"No, it's not really that. Denton Morrison came up with it. One of his publicity gambits. I think it was the whole Australian thing, and maybe because I'm known in the league for spending a lot of time in the penalty box."

"Does that mean you play too rough?"

"I can play rough when it's called for. Mostly it's because I get so passionate about the game. Sometimes my emotions get the better of me."

"It doesn't sound as if Denton thinks that's a bad thing."

"Nah. The fans like it."

He laughed. "It is funny, when you think about it— the Man Tamer and the Wild Man. Sounds like one of those crazy wrestling teams or something."

"Yeah. Or something."

5

Man-Taming Principle One: Teach By Example. In order for your man to know the kind of behavior you want from him, you must model that behavior for him. In other words, if you want lots of hugs and kisses, give lots of hugs and kisses. If you want him to swear less, be sure to watch your own language. If there's something in particular you want from him in bed, then show him. This principle should be carried out in a very nonjudgmental, almost matter-of-fact manner. It's not about what he's doing wrong—it's about what pleases you.

RACHEL SURVEYED the chaotic scene in the gymnasium of the Vickery Meadows Boys and Girls Club: while a group of boys shot hoops at one end of the cavernous space, a group of girls raced around the gym, squealing at top volume. A third set of children booted a dodge ball back and forth while a fourth set of kids whacked at each other with lacrosse sticks. Garret stood in the middle of this last group, and as Rachel stared, he put one boy in a headlock and ruffled his hair, all the while addressing the other boys, who'd stopped hitting each other long enough to watch their playmate struggle to free himself from Garret's grasp.

Thweeet! A deafening whistle pierced Rachel's eardrums and a very tall, very thin woman wearing gym shorts and a tank top strode to the middle of the gym. "Listen up, everybody!" she shouted in the sudden quiet. "Mr. Kelly is here to teach you about lacrosse, so shut up and pay attention."

All eyes swiveled to Garret, who released his captive and joined the woman at the center of the room. He carried a lacrosse stick in one hand, a small rubber ball in the other. "Thanks, Ms. Ellie," he said, and began bouncing the ball. The ball hit the gym floor hard— *thwack*—then returned to his hand. Both the sound and the repetitive movement were mesmerizing. The children and Rachel continued to stare as if under a spell.

"Do you all know what you get if you cross a snake with a kangaroo?" he asked, still bouncing the ball.

"No!" one boy shouted.

Garret looked up from the ball, one eyebrow lifted in mock disbelief that they did not know the answer to such a simple question. "Why, you get a jump rope, of course."

It was a stupid joke, but everyone, including Rachel, howled with laughter.

"All right then, let's get down to it." Garret stopped bouncing the ball. "My name's Garret Kelly and I play for the Dallas Devils, a new indoor lacrosse team here in town, and I'm here today to show you a few things about the game."

A pigtailed girl on the front row stuck up a timid

hand. Garret nodded to her. "Did you have a question, miss?"

"Are you from Australia?" she asked.

"That I am, my dear. You can ask questions about that later. Now to lacrosse." He held up the ball. "Lacrosse is played with a ball like this and a stick like this." He hefted the stick. "You'll see the stick has a net on the end of it in which you can catch the ball." He tossed up the ball and demonstrated catching it with the stick. "You can also throw the ball—or pass it to another player—with the stick." With a flick of his wrist the ball flew out, bounced against the opposite wall and rolled back toward him. A small boy pounced on it, grinning, and handed it back to Garret.

"All right now, I want you all to line up next to me here and we'll take turns practicing handling the stick."

Rachel helped Ms. Ellie arrange the children in some semblance of order and for the next hour Garret showed children how to hold the lacrosse stick, and use it to throw and catch the ball. He dodged flailing sticks and flying balls, coaxed timid children and calmed overly excited ones. Rachel did her best to maintain order while keeping her eye on Garret as much as possible.

He was a great teacher, patient and full of praise. While dealing with so many children was exhausting to her, he seemed energized by the experience. And the children loved him. When it was time for him to leave they lined up to exchange hugs or, in the case of the more macho boys, fist bumps with him.

He met up with Rachel at the door on the far side of

the gym. "You were great," she said. "The children adored you."

"They're not a bad lot," he said. "Some of them might even make decent lacrosse players one day."

"Is that why you're doing this?" she asked. "To train future players?"

"Nah, I like kids." He grinned. "Plus it's a good excuse to act like one myself."

She smiled. "Yes, you're good at that." Not that that was necessarily a bad thing.... A tinny rendition of Vivaldi interrupted her. She retrieved her cell phone from her purse and answered it.

"Rachel, where are you?" Denton Morrison never bothered with a traditional greeting, as if to remind everyone that he was a busy, important man who couldn't waste his time on such niceties.

If not for the bet, Rachel would have told him it was none of his business, but she wanted him to know she was on the job and he needed to keep that afternoon programming slot open for her. "I'm with Garret Kelly," she said. "We're just leaving the Vickery Meadows Boys and Girls Club."

"You didn't waste any time latching onto him, did you?" Denton said. "Well, it doesn't matter. You're still going to lose the bet."

"I don't think so," she said, trying to hide her annoyance. She glanced at Garret. He was busy stowing the lacrosse gear in the back of his truck. She walked a little way away, out of earshot. "He doesn't know about our bet and I'd appreciate it if you didn't tell him."

"Why not? Afraid it will skew the odds in his favor?"

"No. But this is between you and me. He doesn't need to know." Besides, the whole idea behind her principles was that the man didn't know about them. That was the beauty of her program.

"Fine," Denton said. "I'll keep quiet for now. Let me talk to him."

"I thought you called me. Why do you need to talk to Garret?"

"This concerns both of you. But as long as he's there, I want to talk to him first."

No doubt another one of Denton's great ideas for publicity. She gritted her teeth and took a deep breath, struggling for calm. "You won't say anything about our bet?"

"Don't you worry about me. You worry about him."

She walked back to the truck and handed the phone to Garret. "It's Denton. He wants to talk to you."

If he was surprised Denton knew they were together, he didn't show it. "Called to tell me again what a great job I did last night, did you?" he said.

But his jovial expression transformed to a frown as he listened to whatever Denton had to say. "No, mate. I don't like the idea at all," he said after a moment.

Another long pause while Denton talked. Rachel studied Garret's face for some clue as to what was going on. His scowl deepened and her tiny phone all but disappeared in his white-knuckled grip. "That's crazy," he said. Then after a short pause. "You're going too far. I won't do it." And finally. "If you don't like it, you can take it up with my agent."

He flipped the phone shut and handed it back to Rachel. "That boss of yours is a pain in the arse," he said.

"He's your boss, too, isn't he?"

"More's the pity." He opened the passenger door of the truck and held it while she climbed in. "How did he know you were with me?" he asked.

"When I answered the phone, he asked where I was and I told him." She shrugged. "Then he said he wanted to talk to you. What did he say?"

He shut the door and walked around to the driver's side and climbed in. "He wants the two of us to make a half-time appearance at the Mavericks game tonight."

"That's the basketball team, right?"

He laughed. "You really don't follow sports, do you? Yes, it's the basketball team. Denton owns them, too."

"What does he want us to do?"

He started the engine and backed out of the parking space. "Just show up courtside. He's going to feed something to the local gossip columnists so they'll make it big in the local rags. He's very keen on playing up the whole Wild Man and the Man Tamer angle."

"But you told him no."

"Damn right I told him no." His eyes met hers, his look full of meaning. "I have plans for tonight and they don't include posing for the photogs at a basketball game."

"Plans?" Her mouth went dry, contemplating what those plans might be.

He nodded. "Big plans."

MOIRA STARED AT THE PHONE, trying to work up the courage to pick it up and punch in David's number. She'd promised herself she'd get serious about putting

Rachel's man-taming principles to work. David was the man she loved. The man she wanted to spend the rest of her life with. All she had to do was change a few of his bad habits and they could have the perfect relationship she'd always wanted.

She took a deep breath, picked up the receiver and punched the speed-dial button for David's number. He answered on the second ring. A good sign, she thought. That meant he wasn't already involved in some televised sporting event.

Either that, or she'd caught him during a commercial.

"Hey, honey," she said. "How are you?"

"I'm good. What's up?"

"I was hoping I could talk you into coming over to my place for dinner tonight." She dropped her voice to a sexy purr.

"That sounds great."

She pumped her arm in a silent victory celebration. Score one for successfully distracting him from an evening in front of the TV. This could be the start of a new phase in their relationship. She'd wow him with a gourmet dinner, then slip into that sexy negligee she'd bought last week and make him forget all about basketball, football, baseball or any balls but the ones between his legs.

"But why don't you come over here instead?"

Her fantasies for a perfect evening came crashing to the ground. She swallowed hard. "Why don't you want to come over to my place?" Did he not like her apartment? Was her bedroom too feminine? Did he have some never-before-voiced objection to her cat?

"Your place is great. But I've got a big-screen TV and the Mavericks are playing tonight."

"The idea is for us to have a romantic evening together. Just the two of us. Without basketball."

Her obvious anger was enough to make him back off a little. "I'm not talking about watching the game," he said. "I could just turn it on every once in a while to check the score. And you could still cook here."

"You own exactly one frying pan and one saucepan. I can't cook a real meal with that."

"Why not? I do it all the time."

"Mac and cheese and frozen pizza are not real meals."

"Aw, honey, don't be that way."

"Be what way?"

"Upset. What's the big deal about eating dinner here instead of at your place? Relationships are about compromise, right?"

She hated when he pretended to be so reasonable, when in reality he was anything but. "That means both people compromise, not just me," she said. "Sometimes I think you love sports more than you love me."

"That's not true. You just never give sports a chance."

"How can you say that?" She swallowed angry tears. She had to remain calm. Keep the upper hand. "Rachel and I went to a Dallas Devils lacrosse game last night."

"You did?" Should she be flattered or dismayed that the news excited him so much? "You should have invited me."

"It was a girls' night out," she said.

"So what did you think? Did you have a good time?"

"Yeah, it was fun." The game had been exciting and fast-paced. Even when she hadn't been sure what was going on, she hadn't been bored. "We even met some of the players afterward. They were really good-looking."

She hoped her comment might make him jealous, but no such luck. "Did you talk to Wild Man Kelly?" Dave asked. "He's amazing."

"Yes, I talked to him, and to some of the other players. Now about dinner…"

"You don't have to go to all the trouble of cooking for me," he said. "I'll take you out. Somewhere nice. We can go early and be back here in time for the game. If you like lacrosse, I'm sure you'd learn to love basketball."

I don't want to love basketball. I only want to love you. But the words stuck in her throat, behind a knot of tears. "No thanks. I'd rather stay home."

"Okay. We can get together some other night," he said.

"Yeah, whenever you can fit me into your schedule." She hung up, then stared at the phone, gulping tears, waiting for him to call back. All he had to do was apologize, and maybe plead for her to forgive him.

But the phone remained stubbornly silent.

So much for her prowess as a man tamer. All she'd done was screw things up worse.

AT THE DOOR to Garret's apartment, he and Rachel were greeted by frantic barking. "Better stand clear," Garret said as he grasped the doorknob. "Barney's a mite enthusiastic with his greetings."

"So I gather," Rachel said, remembering her muddied dress from that morning. She stepped behind Garret just in time, as Barney came barreling toward them. He planted his front feet on Garret's chest and deposited a wet doggy kiss on his cheek.

"Down, boy," Garret said, and shoved the dog back into the apartment.

As Barney's front feet hit the floor, he realized Rachel was there and bounced up again to greet her. She managed to duck behind Garret again. "Maybe you should try tranquilizers," she said.

"He'll be right as rain after a walk." Garret took a leash from a hook by the door and held it up. "C'mon, boy. Want to go walkies?"

Barney leaped into the air again, almost doing a backflip in his exuberance. Garret somehow managed to snap on the leash and the dog dragged him out the door. "You coming?" Garret called to Rachel.

She shrugged. "Sure." Either that or stay behind in Garret's messy apartment, fighting the twin compulsions to clean and snoop.

They ran most of the first block, Barney loping in the lead, dragging Garret who, no doubt thanks to hours of running up and down lacrosse courts, kept up with no problem. Rachel brought up the rear, huffing and puffing, trying to ignore the stitch developing in her side.

"What's the matter?" Garret asked when they stopped at the corner. "You sound winded."

"I'm not…a runner," she said, bracing herself against the stop sign and holding her side.

"You should try it. It's great for your stamina."

"I'll…be fine." She'd be great as soon as she was

back in her own clothes, drinking a martini and watching the travel channel. Now *that* was a great way to spend an afternoon, not racing some drooling beast around the block.

Unless, of course, the beast in question had six-pack abs, buns of steel and was drooling after her. She glanced at Garret. Except for the drool, he definitely qualified. She straightened and sucked in a bracing breath. All right then. Maybe this wasn't a waste of time after all.

By the time they headed back toward the apartment, Barney had slowed to a brisk walk and Rachel was secure in the knowledge that her previous decision not to participate in any marathons, ever, had been the right choice.

As had her decision to never own dogs. As she headed toward the stairs to Garret's front door, Barney lifted his leg and narrowly missed peeing on her shoes. "Why would anyone want to own an animal like that?" she asked as Garret unlocked the door.

"Dogs are great," he said. "I can't imagine not having one." He unsnapped the leash and Barney raced into the kitchen. Seconds later a sound like waves slapping against a boat dock reached their ears as the dog no doubt drained his water dish.

"Well, maybe a little one would be all right," she said. "One of those I could carry around in my purse." One that wasn't large enough to knock her down and take off all her makeup with one swipe of its tongue.

"You are such a girly girl." He laughed and went into the kitchen.

She followed him. "I didn't hear you complaining last night," she said.

He opened the refrigerator and took out two beers, and handed one to her. She started to tell him she wasn't much for beer, but the chilled glass bottle in her hand felt good, and suddenly the idea of a cold brew sounded even better. "I'm not complaining now," he said. "I think it's cute."

"To quote Susan Sarandon, 'baby ducks are cute,'" she said. "Grown women don't aspire to cuteness."

"All right then, you're beautiful. And fun to be with."

She blushed. After all, she hadn't really been fishing for a compliment. "Thanks."

He poured kibble into Barney's bowl. "Let's go into the living room where it's more comfortable," he said.

He sank onto the black leather sofa and patted the spot beside him. "Come here and tell me about this man-taming stuff."

Uh-oh. Her stomach lurched. Time for the delicate male ego to object to the idea that he could be persuaded to do anything that wasn't his idea in the first place. These conversations never went well. Would she lose yet another promising relationship—and her bet with Denton—before she'd even started?

She took a long swallow of liquid courage, then set the bottle on the coffee table. "The man taming name is just a catchy marketing angle," she said. "It's really about behavior modification. By using various techniques such as positive reinforcement people can change behavior, overcome phobias and eliminate bad habits."

"So you teach women how to use this behavior modification stuff to get rid of their guys' bad habits?"

"You got it." She opened her hands wide. "Nothing sneaky or weird about it."

He nodded, a mock serious expression on his face. "A woman would never act sneaky or weird."

She punched his shoulder. "And a man would never be sarcastic or rude."

"Me? Sarcastic?" He laughed. "So tell me about these *various techniques.* I want to know what I should be on the lookout for, in case you get any ideas about changing me."

"It's not about changing you," she said. "It's about changing behavior." And he was crazy if he thought she was going to tell him all her secrets. If he was so curious, he could read her column in the magazine. Though the one man who had taken her up on that offer had dropped her like a scorching steel ball bearing. "It's all very boring, dry psychological stuff anyway," she added. She picked up the remote control—a sure tactic for diverting a guy's attention. "Let's see what's on TV."

Garret took the remote from her. "Don't try to change the subject. I'm really interested here. You must know something if half the women in Dallas are reading your column."

"Two-thirds, actually, according to the latest surveys."

"There you go. So tell me about these techniques."

She was tempted to lie, if only for self-protection. But lies were easy to disprove and, besides, it was nice to meet a man who was genuinely interested in her work. She didn't have to tell him *everything,* she reasoned. Only enough to satisfy his curiosity.

"All right. Well, the first principle to getting anyone to do what you want is to teach by example. You need to *show* them exactly the behavior you desire from them."

He nodded. "Makes sense. A bloke can't be expected to know what to do if he doesn't have an example to follow."

"Not all the time, of course, but certainly sometimes."

"So give me an example. A situation where you'd give me an example to follow and I'd do it."

She started to point out that if he knew what she wanted ahead of time he could always opt to refuse out of sheer obstinacy to follow her example. But the whole point, of course, was to make him want to follow her example regardless of his own resistance. And there was one situation where this almost always worked.

She smiled, impressed by her own brilliance. She shifted into a more comfortable position on the sofa, facing him, with one leg tucked under her. "All right. For instance, therapists and counselors are always telling women that men aren't mind readers in the bedroom. If a woman wants something, she needs to tell him. Or better yet, show him."

"Is that so?" Amazing how one quirk of an eyebrow could raise the temperature in the room ten degrees. "Why don't you show me what *you* want?"

"Right now?" The idea excited her. She glanced around the room. Barney snored on a dog bed in the corner but otherwise all was silent. "Right here?"

He set his beer aside and leaned back. "Why not? I'm not going anywhere. Are you?"

Oh yeah, she was going somewhere all right. She was taking a thrill ride with The Wild Man. And she wasn't in any hurry for the ride to stop.

6

Man Taming in the Bedroom

Some of the Man Tamer's critics have charged that man taming constitutes nothing more than a woman using sex to manipulate a man and get what she wants. Anyone who thinks this has not been paying attention. Man taming is about behavior modification and retraining. It focuses on the whole relationship—not merely what happens in the bedroom. While it may at times be appropriate to apply man-taming principles in the bedroom, sex is not to be used to bully your partner into compliance. To do so distorts the entire foundation of man taming, which is designed to build a more well-rounded relationship, both in and out of the bedroom.

SHOW ME WHAT YOU WANT. The words hovered between them, ripe with possibility. What *did* she want? And how to demonstrate that for him? Rachel closed her eyes, gathering her thoughts. She'd never been challenged to define her desires so precisely and struggled against self-consciousness.

When she opened her eyes again she met Garret's gaze. His look was warm and encouraging. "I'm ready when you are," he said.

She nodded, and wet her suddenly dry lips. "I'm trying to think where to begin," she confessed.

"Show me where you like to be touched. And show me how."

His words—and the possibilities they conveyed—sent a warm shiver through her, driving out her hesitation. She brought her hands up to rest on either side of her neck. "I like to be touched here, where the skin of my neck is especially soft and sensitive." She brushed her fingers beneath her jaw, sparks of sensation skittering through her at even this light touch.

"And how do you like to be touched?" he asked.

"With your hands." She stared at his lips and remembered the feel of them on her. "And your mouth. And your tongue." Her skin tingled with anticipation of just such touches from him.

She slid her hands down her neck to her shoulders, then over her breasts, less hesitant to express herself now. She could see how she was turning him on, in the way his pupils dilated and the increased rhythm of his breathing. "When I'm aroused, my breasts ache to be touched," she said. "To be held and fondled and kissed." She pressed her palms against the hard tips of her nipples, which she could feel now through the shirt and bra.

Garret nodded, and shifted to face her more, his legs apart, eyes fixed on her. "Show me," he said, his voice low. Urgent.

She closed her eyes again and cupped her breasts in her hands, feeling their roundness and heaviness. She traced one finger around the curve of one, moving in a spiral, slowly drawing closer to the sensitive nipple. She raked her nail across that hard bud and gasped at the sharp desire that speared her.

She opened her eyes again and saw her own need reflected in his dark pupils, her struggle for composure echoed in his labored breathing. She slid her hands down her torso, then out to her hips. "I like it when a man takes the time to appreciate all of me," she said. "My stomach and my hips and thighs. All those places I don't always love myself."

"All those places where a woman is wonderfully different from a man," he said.

She smiled. "I hadn't really thought of it that way."

"I appreciate every part of you," he said. He nodded. "Go on."

She rested her hands on the insides of her thighs, taking a moment to focus on the tension building between her legs. She was hot and tight, on edge with wanting. The earthy scent of her arousal rose up between them.

She slid one finger beneath the edge of her shorts, stroking along the leg of her panties, feeling her pulse jump in response. "I like it when a man postpones his own gratification in favor of mine."

He smiled. "You like to come first."

"Sometimes." She slid the finger up farther, under the elastic. "And sometimes I just want to be ready, to be almost there when he enters me." She parted her folds and found the hard nub of her clit. "I like to be stroked here. With your fingers. And your tongue. Especially your tongue." She grew still, feeling the beat of her pulse against her finger, letting the tension build.

Eyes locked to hers, Garret leaned toward her. "Take your clothes off," he said, his voice a low growl.

She managed a shaky breath, and a shakier smile. "You first."

IF IT WAS POSSIBLE for a man to be half mad with lust, Garret reasoned he was almost there. His hands shook as he grasped the hem of his shirt and tugged it over his head. The shirt went sailing, followed by shorts and boxers.

Rachel watched him, not moving, her gaze akin to a physical touch, roaming across his body. His nipples hardened and his penis, already erect, jerked in anticipation.

He leaned toward her, reaching for her, but she leaned back and stripped off her own shirt, shorts and underwear. He'd wanted her to leave the bra and panties on, so that he could remove them, like unwrapping a package.

But this wasn't about what he wanted, he reminded himself. This was all about her wants. What she needed from him.

When she was naked, she lay back against the sofa pillows. "Do you want to go into the bedroom?" she asked.

"Do you?"

She shook her head. "No. I want you right here."

"You've got me." He rose and rested one knee between her legs, bracing himself with one foot on the floor as he leaned in closer and kissed her full on the mouth. "Don't go away," he said. "I'll be right back."

He went into the bedroom and retrieved a condom from the nightstand drawer. When he returned to the living room, she had not changed position at all. He knelt between her legs once more and kissed the soft skin at the underside of her neck. The faint scent of her perfume mingled with the musk of arousal, an intoxicating blend that made his heart race.

He trailed his tongue along the curve of her jaw, then moved down to kiss her collarbone. She felt as delicate as a bird, yet there was nothing fragile in the way she arched to him, or the way her arms encircled and held him.

He trailed kisses to the tops of her breasts, then cupped his hands around her, enjoying the weight of her in his palms, the scrape of her erect nipples against his skin.

When he bent again to take one nipple in his mouth she moaned. The sound sent a fresh, sharper rush of desire through him, and he slid his hands to her waist and pulled her tighter against him, even as his mouth remained locked to her breast.

He alternately suckled and teased with his tongue, until she was writhing beneath him, incoherent little pants and moans urging him on.

He moved to her other breast and lavished it with attention. Rachel's hands alternately smoothed and raked his back. He felt the jut of her hipbones against his palms as he held her, and the heat of her mons as she arched against his belly.

He was sorely tempted to move straight to satisfying the silent pleading of that pressure against his belly, but forced himself to move slowly. To take his time to appreciate all of her, as she had asked.

He slid his hands beneath her to cup her bottom. "You have a gorgeous ass," he said, squeezing gently. "Just watching you walk away is enough to make me lose my train of thought."

"Is that so?" She smiled weakly. "I'll have to remember that."

"Now I've told you my secret. I'm putty in your hands."

She surprised a gasp from him when she reached down and grabbed hold of his erection. "This doesn't feel like putty to me."

"No. Not putty." He lowered his head again and kissed her soft belly, then slid down farther and traced the juncture of her thigh with his tongue. Her skin was like hot satin, the anticipation of burying himself in such luxury making coherent thought impossible.

He parted her folds with his fingers, then followed with his tongue. She gasped and jerked against him and he put one hand flat on her stomach, urging her to hold still. He traced her entrance with his tongue, then slid two fingers into her, feeling her muscles contract around him, and a corresponding contraction in his own groin.

He tasted the tang of her arousal, his tongue stroking fast, then slow. She buried her fingers in his hair and clutched him to her. "Yes," she breathed. "Yes!"

He sensed her impending climax in the increased tension of her muscles and the frantic rhythm of her breathing. He stroked harder and was rewarded with a keening cry and the arch of her body against him. She wrapped her legs around him and slid her hands to his shoulders as he continued to caress her with his tongue.

"Come up here," she gasped. "I want you in me."

He sheathed himself with the condom, then grasped her hips and shifted her around so that both her feet were on the floor and he was able to straddle her, his hands braced on the back of the sofa for leverage.

She was hot and slick, and sinking into her was the only paradise he needed to know. She took him fully and when he withdrew partway she reached around and grasped his buttocks and pulled him to her once more.

"Don't worry, I'm not leaving," he said through clenched teeth, fighting for control. She had him so turned on he feared he might go off before they'd even started. But her hand on the back of his neck and her mouth on his cooled his fever for a moment. He focused on the tenderness of the gesture, the softness of her lips, the sweetness of her tongue. When he finally drew back to look into her eyes once more, anticipation began to build anew, no longer frantic, but full of excitement at the thought of what lay before them.

He began to move in a slow, smooth rhythm, sinking into her completely before withdrawing partway. She rose up to meet him, her hands on his buttocks and back, eyes open, staring at him with silent encouragement and building heat.

His climax hit him hard, a runaway train he couldn't stop. She dug her fingers into his backside, taking him more fully inside her, moving with him until he was fully sated.

He collapsed against her, hugging her to him, his cheek resting against hers, eyes closed, waiting for his breathing to slow. When he was finally able to form words, he said, "Woman, I am slain. You've demonstrated your man-taming prowess."

She laughed, and smoothed her hands down his back. "I don't know that I'm in a hurry for the Wild Man to be tamed in bed."

He withdrew from her and helped her lie back on the sofa, then he lay beside her, his head nestled against her shoulder. "The Wild Man is on hiatus," he said. He brought his hand up to cover her breast. "But give him a few hours and we could arrange a return engagement."

"Mmm. I could get to like this combination of tamed and wild."

And he could get to like spending time with her. Pleasing her. In a more rational frame of mind, the idea might have frightened him. But there was nothing rational about lust, or about love, for that matter. He didn't care to examine how close the two feelings could be to one another.

RACHEL WAS SCARCELY OUT of bed the next morning before the phone rang. "Have you seen the paper?" Rhonda asked without preamble.

Rachel made a face and refilled her coffee cup. "No. I never have time to read it. Was your picture in it?"

"No. There was a mention in the Talk of the Town column about the Winter Fantasy ball, but that's not why I'm calling."

"So why are you calling? Or are we going to play

guessing games?" She sat at the kitchen table and stirred sugar into her coffee.

"Don't be sarcastic," Rhonda said. "I'm calling because there's a very embarrassing item in that same column about you dating some lacrosse player named Wild Man."

Rachel laughed. So Denton's publicity plan was working. "Garret Kelly. I told you about him. He plays lacrosse for the Dallas Devils."

"I know. What are you doing dating him?"

"Because I like him. And he likes me. What does the paper say about us?"

She heard the rattle of newspaper, then Rhonda said, "It's in Talk of the Town, with the heading 'Wild Man Meets Man Tamer.' It says, 'Dallas Devils' star Garret "Wild Man" Kelly has been seen about town in the company of none other than *Belinda* magazine columnist Rachel Westover, aka "the Man Tamer." Ms. Westover's popular column purports to teach women how to domesticate the men in their lives. But will her techniques work on this sexy Australian import, who is said to live up to his nickname both on and off the lacrosse court?'"

Rachel smiled. "It says my column is popular. I like that."

"The Man Tamer and the Wild Man?" Rhonda's voice rose. "Don't you find that the least bit embarrassing?"

"It's just a publicity angle Denton Morrison is playing up. He thinks any publicity is good publicity and he wants as much as he can get for this new lacrosse team."

"But what do *you* think about it?"

"I think it's pretty funny. And I guess it might pull in a few more readers for my column."

"If you don't care about your own reputation, at least think of mine," Rhonda whined.

Rachel rolled her eyes. "Oh please. You're Miss Do-Gooder of the Decade. Nothing I do is going to mar your pristine image."

"Do you think I'm too uptight?" Rhonda asked.

"Of course. But that's never bothered you before."

Rhonda didn't answer right away. Rachel felt a pang of guilt. Maybe she'd gone too far this time. Maybe she'd really hurt Rhonda's feelings. "Rhonda, I—" she began.

But her sister interrupted her. "This morning I told Harrison I was thinking of going in costume as the Frost Queen to the Winter Fantasy ball," Rhonda said. "He acted as if that wasn't a good idea."

Rachel winced. "It will give your enemies plenty to talk about," she said.

"I don't have any enemies." Rhonda's voice grew strident once more. It was probably true. The woman bent over backward to stay in everyone's good graces. Except, of course, her sister's.

"Then you're definitely doing something wrong," Rachel said. "Did Harrison suggest any alternative costumes?"

"He suggested something more daring. He said he'd like to show me off."

"That's really sweet." Maybe Harrison wasn't such a stick-in-the-mud after all.

"I always swore I wouldn't be the typical trophy wife," Rhonda said. "I've worked hard to show the world I'm not some dumb blonde who married him for his money and social position. Now he wants me to negate all that by dressing like a bimbo."

"Not like a bimbo," Rachel said, her voice gentle. "Maybe all he wants is for you to loosen up a little. So he can show the world the softer side of you he loves. There's nothing wrong with that."

"Maybe." Rhonda's voice was strained and she sniffed. Rachel wondered if her sister was *crying.* "I refuse to dress like a slut," Rhonda said.

"Just rethink the Frost Queen business. Wait—I know! You can play up the whole 'cold as ice' thing and go as a dominatrix, except all in white! The *real* Frost Queen."

"That is the most ridiculous thing I've ever heard."

Rachel grinned. "I bet Harrison would like it. And you still have the figure for it." She wished *she* was in as good a shape as her sister.

"No. That's…disgusting."

"Oh, lighten up! It's a costume ball. Have some fun."

"A dominatrix is not my idea of fun."

"Well, hosting charity balls is not my idea of fun."

"It's for a very worthy cause."

"Yeah, yeah, yeah, but what have you done lately that's really *fun?*"

"Harrison and I vacationed in the Azores last June."

"Did you wear a bikini? Or better yet, sunbathe topless?"

"No! I had a very nice maillot from Anne Cole."

"You'd have had more fun in a bikini. And you'd have *definitely* had more fun topless."

"Is that the kind of advice you give your man tamer readers?"

"No, it's the kind of advice I give my friends."

Considering their often-antagonistic relationship, Rachel was surprised by her own words, but she meant them. Rhonda could be a lot of fun, if she'd just loosen up a little.

Rhonda was apparently surprised, too. There was another long silence, then she said, "I'll think about the costume some more. Maybe I can find a compromise. In the meantime, I want to know more about this Wild Man person. Is it serious between the two of you?"

Of course Rhonda would always bring the conversation back around to Rachel and what she was doing wrong in her life. "Garret and I are friends," she said.

"Just friends?"

Her grin now was positively wicked. Too bad Rhonda couldn't see her face. "Friends with benefits."

"What does that mean?"

"If you can't figure it out, I'm not going to explain it."

"Rachel, are you sure it's wise to sleep with a man you hardly know?"

Rachel sighed. "I'm not going to discuss this anymore. I have to get to work now. Goodbye." She hung up. That would give Rhonda something to think about.

But her sister's final question stuck with her. What did wisdom have to do with romantic relationships? If she'd been *wise* she never would have taken Denton's stupid bet in the first place. She'd have found another way to get the television show she wanted.

But she was in too deep to go back now.

7
_____

Man-Taming Principle Two: Reward Good Behavior.

One of the cornerstones of behavior modification is the use of positive reinforcement. Right behavior leads to rewards, in the form of praise, affection and other positive responses. This is one of the most effective, and most pleasant, training techniques.

If your guy is a natural slob, yet he cleans up his place for your visit, you can reinforce this behavior by thanking him, complimenting him and being extra affectionate. Both of you win in this situation.

Remember, change doesn't happen overnight. You will probably have to start with reinforcing small behaviors, such as picking up clothes from the floor or making the bed. The goal is to move in steps until the end results—a clean apartment— is reached. Stay positive and have fun with it.

TEACHING BY EXAMPLE had definitely brought their relationship to the next level, Rachel thought. At least in the bedroom. And her attempts at positive reinforcement seemed to be working, too. She'd been gratified to see on her most recent visit to Garret's apartment that he had changed the sheets and made the bed. Time to increase her efforts in that area and to build on her previous success.

The Devils had an off week, so Rachel offered to cook dinner for Garret at her apartment. He arrived on time and she was quick to praise him for that.

"Years of traveling to practices and games have taught me to be punctual," he said. He shrugged out of his jacket and draped it over the back of a chair.

"I love that shirt," she said, smoothing her hand across the front of his dark blue button-down. "The color brings out your eyes." She avoided looking at his pants, which were an odd shade of green that didn't go with the shirt at all. They could work on coordinating clothes some other time.

"You look hot in this dress." He pulled her close, his hands sliding down the red silk to rest at the small of her back. He kissed her, a long, passionate kiss that made her head spin. "I can't wait to get it off you."

She laughed and pushed him away. "It's tempting, but I think we should have dinner before dessert. Would you open the wine?" She pointed to the bottle she'd set out on the bar and went to check on the rice.

"Australian wine," he said, admiring the label. "Good choice." He manipulated the corkscrew, struggling a little with the cork. "Damn plastic things never want to come out." He grunted, finally freeing the cork. "Oops, spilled a little." He grabbed one of her best dishcloths off the hook by the stove and started to wipe up the spill.

Rachel intercepted him just in time. "Use a paper towel," she said, handing him a couple of sheets.

He poured two glasses of wine and handed one to her. "To the Man Tamer and the Wild Man," he said.

She laughed. "I take it you saw the item in the newspaper."

"Saw it? It was taped to my locker when I showed up for practice last night. The guys have given me no end of hell about it."

"You seem to be holding up all right."

He laughed. "I think it's a riot. And I don't think I'm in any danger of being tamed anytime soon." His look telegraphed just how wild his thoughts of her were.

She suppressed a smug smile of her own. The beauty of man taming, she could have told him, is that the man never realizes what's happening until it's too late. She turned to the stove. "Dinner's ready. Why don't you have a seat and I'll bring it out."

The food was simple—a chicken and rice dish with a spicy flair, broccoli and store-bought rolls. Garret heaped his plate full and ate with relish. "This is delicious," he raved. "Best meal I've had in weeks."

"Thanks," she said. "I do all right in the kitchen, but I'm not a fancy cook. Now my sister, Rhonda, she's a regular gourmet chef. She's taken all these classes and has shelves full of cookbooks."

"I'm more of a meat-and-two-veg man myself. I'm not all that into fancy food."

"I guess when you travel you have the opportunity to eat in a lot of great restaurants," she said.

He laughed. "You'd guess wrong. Half the time the

plane gets in late and we have to settle for grabbing a burger on the way to the hotel. Or if we're lucky the kitchen wherever we're staying will still be open and we can order room service, which can be dicey at times." He wagged his fork at her. "The life of the professional lacrosse player is not all glamour and pretty girls," he said drolly.

She couldn't remember when a man had made her laugh so much. "When is the next game?" she asked.

"We're going to Portland next Friday." He took a sip of wine. "I was hoping I could talk you into looking after Barney for me while I'm away."

She froze, a forkful of rice halfway to her mouth. He wanted her to be alone with that Mack truck of a dog? For a whole weekend? She set the fork aside. "How can I do that? My apartment doesn't allow dogs." And no telling what the beast would do to her furniture.

"You could go by a couple times a day to feed him and take him for a walk. Or you're welcome to stay at my place."

Stay at his apartment without him there? Not unless it was disinfected first. She didn't want to think what she might find under the bed or hidden in closets.

In spite of her horror, she was also touched. "You'd trust me that much?" she asked.

"Sure. I know you'll take good care of him."

She hadn't been referring to the dog. Didn't Garret realize that a woman left alone in his apartment would be compelled to snoop? The urge to learn his secrets was practically a genetic mandate.

"Besides, Barney really likes you," he said.

She gulped more wine. "He does? How can you tell?"

"He's always thrilled to see you. He's never that eager with anyone else."

No doubt the dog sensed how uncomfortable she was with him and went out of his way to take advantage of that. As flattered as she was by Garret's request, and as much as she wanted to help him out, she was still searching for a way to gracefully get out of this particular obligation. "Who took care of him before you met me?" she asked.

"I had a pet sitter come in, but the guy's moved away. I hate to have a stranger coming in. That's why I thought you'd be the perfect solution."

His pleading look made it impossible for her to say no. "Sure." What was going over to his place a couple of times a day for a couple of days to look after one dog? Maybe she could get Moira to help. Then at least it would be two against one.

Garret helped her with the dishes. As they scraped plates and rinsed silverware, she thought how well they worked together. She smiled as she imagined what Denton would think if he could see them now. His Wild Man was already fairly well domesticated.

"I was thinking of going to the movies tomorrow night," she said as she rinsed the last plate and handed it to him to dry. "Want to come with me?"

"Can't. It's my poker night."

"Poker?" She tried not to let her disappointment show.

"Yeah, a bunch of guys from the team get together once a month to play. It's coed though. You could come, too."

Not her idea of a fun evening. "I don't know how to play poker," she said.

"Then it's time you learned. Do you have any cards?"

She started to tell him she had no interest in learning. Especially not now, when she'd been looking forward to *dessert*. "You want to play cards now?" she asked.

"You'll love it. You'll see."

She would never understand the way men's minds worked. When he'd arrived he couldn't wait to get her dress off, now all he could think about was some stupid card game. But she told herself it was always good to explore new things. Besides, this probably fell under the category of teaching by example. If she was a good sport about participating in things he enjoyed, she could remind him of this when it came time for him to take her to the ballet or something similar.

She dug around in her desk until she found a deck of cards she'd received as a freebie from one of the advertisers at the magazine.

"All right." He walked over to the coffee table and lowered himself to the floor. "Come over here and let's get started."

She watched, amused, as he shuffled the cards. Any minute now she expected him to suggest a game of strip poker—which sounded much more interesting to her right now than the conventional variety. But apparently poker was serious business to Garret.

He cut the deck, then dealt five cards to each of them. "All right then, poker is a simple game. The object is to end up with the highest valued hand. A royal flush is the highest—ten, jack, queen, king and ace, all of the same suit. It's also the toughest hand to get. A straight flush is next in value—any five cards of the same suit in order. Four of a kind is next. That's obvious. Then a full house, flush and a straight, three of a kind, two pair and one pair."

"And you expect me to remember all this?" she asked.

"You'll pick it up in no time, trust me. Now pay attention. We'll go over the rules."

"Rules? Surely you know by now I hate having to play by the rules."

He ignored her teasing and continued in teaching mode. "First, everyone antes—that's the initial bet that everyone puts into the pot. Then the dealer deals five cards to each player, face down. Everybody looks at their hand and makes their bets."

"How much should I bet?"

"How lucky do you feel?" His eyes met his.

She smiled slyly. "Maybe I'm feeling really lucky."

He snorted. "We'll see about that. Let's play and I'll teach you more as we go along."

To her surprise, Rachel won the first hand. And the next. "Beginner's luck," Garret said as he dealt a new hand.

"What, you don't think it's skill?" she teased.

"Luck," he said. "Though I'll admit you've taken to this quickly. Are you sure you've never played before?"

She shook her head. "I haven't liked cards since my sister made me play about a million games of Crazy Eights with her the summer I was twelve. She won almost every hand. I'm sure she cheated, but I could never catch her."

"Gourmet cook and card cheat. This sister of yours sounds like a pistol."

"She can be insufferable. More so since she married three years ago. Her husband has pots of money and is from an old, prestigious Dallas family. Now Rhonda is Ms. High Society, always worried about her image. She's on the board of half a dozen charities and is so busy doing good she doesn't have time to act like a normal person."

"Too bad." He shuffled the cards and began to deal a new hand. "Just as well I've never mingled in high society. I never much cared what people thought of me."

"I keep telling her she needs to loosen up." She glanced at her cards. "Yesterday she was all in a tizzy over what costume to wear to the Winter Fantasy ball. She's the official hostess this year. She actually wanted to go as the Frost Queen." She shook her head. "Considering how stuck up Rhonda can be these days, I told her I didn't think that was such a good idea."

"So what costume would you wear if you were going to this ball?"

She grinned. "I told her she could do the Frost Queen thing if she played it for a joke. Go as a dominatrix, only dressed all in white instead of black. White leather boots, bustier, fishnet hose—that kind of thing."

His eyebrows rose. "I'm thinking I'd like this costume. Tell me more. Would you carry a whip?"

"Absolutely. And everyone would have to address me as 'Your Majesty.'"

"And what about the men who would no doubt flock around you?"

"I'd be as cold and cruel as one would expect from a Frost Queen," she said. "I'd make them kneel at my feet and beg for my attentions."

"And if *I* was one of those men?" he asked.

"I might have to use my whip to keep you in line."

"You'd live up to your reputation as a man tamer, then?"

"Definitely." Her eyes met his, and a thrill shot through her.

"Picturing you with that whip is making me even hotter than that little red dress you're wearing now," he said. He leaned across the table, sweeping the cards aside.

She stood, keeping just out of his reach, and assumed a haughty demeanor. "I could get used to you groveling at my feet this way," she teased, looking down at him.

"Who said anything about groveling, woman?" He reached for her, and pulled her down into his lap. She struggled, but not hard, enjoying the thrill of his strong arms wrapped around her, aroused by the knowledge that he could force her to do anything, but would not.

They rolled together on the carpet, wrestling playfully, hands roaming, caressing, as they pretended to try to escape each other's hold, neither intent on succeeding.

He rolled her over onto her back, his full weight pressing down on her. She writhed beneath him, aware of his erection hard against her pelvis. "You know how to drive a man crazy, don't you?" he growled as he pinned her arms above her head.

Any reply she might have made was cut off by the

pressure of his mouth on hers, his tongue forcing her lips apart, sweeping over her teeth. Play turned to consuming passion as she broke free of his grasp and ripped at his shirt. Buttons flew as she pulled it apart and raked her fingernails down his chest.

He tugged at the hem of her dress, then pulled her into a sitting position and lifted it over her head. With one flick of his fingers he unsnapped her bra and sent it sailing after the dress. He reached for her panties, but she rolled away, laughing as he pursued her on his hands and knees.

He caught her by the sofa and held her by the waist as he stripped off her underwear. Then he slid his hand around to cup her mons while he pressed kisses along her backbone. She was giddy with desire, every touch of his lips sending an electric current of arousal to the tips of her breasts and the hard bud of her clit.

He smoothed his hand down one buttock, squeezing gently, then traced her crack with one finger. One hand still clasping her hip, she heard the slide of his zipper and the rustle of fabric as he removed his pants.

Taking advantage of his distraction, she rolled out of his grasp and leaped to her feet. "Where do you think you're going?" he asked, grabbing her around one leg and pulling himself toward her.

She turned to glare down at him, to make some remark about keeping him in line, but her words were silenced by his mouth on her clit and the firm, wet pressure of his tongue. She caught her breath, dizzy with wanting, and thought her knees would buckle, but he held her firm as he continued to lavish attention on her clit, alternately stroking and sucking, bringing her to the very edge of endurance.

When he released her she stood for a moment, swaying, and stared down at him dumbly. "I'm enjoying this game too much to have it over too soon," he said, grinning.

She shoved hard on his shoulders and he fell back, pulling her along with him. She straddled him, looking down at him, enjoying the view. She traced the line of his jaw, feeling the rough stubble of his beard scrape her palm, then bent and planted a butterfly kiss on the tip of his nose.

"You know I want you very much, don't you?" he said, looking into her eyes.

She nodded. "I want you, too." She pressed her lips to his, then moved quickly down his body, flicking her tongue across his flat brown nipples, trailing kisses down his torso, exploring the indentation of his navel with her tongue.

She smoothed her fingers down the inside of his thighs, then swept upward to cup his balls. He shifted beneath her and his impatience made her smile. She understood not wanting to wait, and yet the waiting itself heightened every sensation.

When she took him in her mouth, he groaned and cupped the back of her head with his hand, smoothing her hair. The gentle intimacy of the gesture and the urgency of his need for her transformed her desire into something more than mere lust and she focused on giving him as much pleasure as he had given her.

She caressed his shaft with her lips and tongue, taking in as much of him as possible, then releasing him oh-so-slowly. The sensation of heated velvet skin over the hard length of him awakened something primal in her. She encircled the base of his shaft with her fingers and began to stroke faster, the tension in her growing as she sensed him nearing his own climax.

When he came she tasted the faint saltiness of his semen and continued to hold him gently in her mouth until he grew still. His fingers twined in her hair, then moved down to caress her shoulders, urging her up.

She slid the length of his body and lay beside him, her thigh draped over his, her head nestled in the hollow of his shoulder. He raised up and looked into her eyes for a long moment, and she had never felt so cherished before. Then he kissed her, a long caress of their lips full of tenderness and passion.

He smoothed his hand over her hips, then urged her onto her back. His lips still locked to hers, he gently parted the folds of her labia and stroked his thumb across her clit. She gasped and arched against him, aching for more.

Using her own wetness for lubrication, he continued to stroke and fondle, varying the speed and pressure of his touch, until she was dancing on the very edge of release, her whole body quivering.

He deepened his kiss and plunged two fingers into her while his thumb continued to stroke across her clit. She came hard, her muscles tensing around him, fingers clutching at him, her body flooding with warmth and weightlessness.

They lay entwined for a long while afterward, eyes closed, not speaking, the only sounds the even rhythm of their breathing. She couldn't remember when she'd had such wild, uninhibited, can't-get-enough-of-you sex, and yet it had been amazingly tender, as well. She loved that Garret could be both gentle and rough, and that he could bring out these sides of her, as well. He was a much more complex person than she would have thought when she first met him.

She'd tell him that one day. When she had the energy.

WHEN RACHEL ARRIVED at Garret's apartment the next night for the big poker party, she wondered at first if she'd wandered into a locker room by mistake. Only the lack of half-naked men and the presence of Garret's sofa—barely discernable under a pile of leather jackets—tipped her off that she was indeed in the right place. Otherwise, who could blame her for confusing the two? Half a dozen men dressed in jerseys or T-shirts were drinking beer and talking lacrosse in loud voices. One even carried a lacrosse stick.

"Come on in and meet the guys." Garret slung an arm around her shoulder and led her into the center of the room. "This is Guy Clifford, Slate Williams and Peter Rutherford. And you remember Bud Mayhew and Tate Maguire. That's Tate's wife, Leslie, and Pamela there is with Guy. Everybody, this is Rachel."

"The Man Tamer!" Tate said, and everyone laughed. Rachel managed to keep a smile on her face as she waited for the inevitable teasing.

"So do you really think you can tame the Wild Man here?" Slate asked.

She pretended to look Garret up and down. He grinned at her, as eager to hear her answer as everyone else. "I think for tonight I'll settle for beating him at poker," she said.

"That sounded like a challenge to me, buddy," Slate said.

"If she plays as good as she looks, could be trouble," someone else said.

Garret laughed and put his arm around Rachel again. "Then we'd best get to it."

While the others arranged tables and pulled out decks of cards and carousels of poker chips, Garret looked at Rachel. "That was a pretty cheeky statement there. Do you really think you can best me tonight?"

Considering she'd only learned to play last night, she figured a snowball had a better chance in hell. But she wasn't one to back down from a challenge, especially one she'd made in front of a bunch of people she'd just met. "Haven't you heard of beginner's luck?"

"Skill beats luck any day, I'd say." He stroked his finger along the underside of her chin, sending a warm tingle through her.

"You think so?"

"Darlin', you don't stand a chance. Best surrender yourself to fate now."

She should have left it there, but such common sense was no match for her pride. She straightened her spine and lifted her chin and said, "Care to bet on that?"

"A wager?" He cocked one eyebrow. "I wouldn't have taken you for a gambling woman."

If he only knew. "I'll bet you twenty dollars that I can beat you at cards tonight."

"Twenty dollars is hardly worth my while."

She swallowed hard. "A hundred then." If she lost, there went her manicure-and-latte funds for a month.

"Forget about money." He bent closer, his breath warm in her ear. "Let's wager something we'd both enjoy more."

"Wh-what did you have in mind?"

"Winner spends the night with the loser."

She laughed. "That's not exactly a hardship on either one of us."

"But…" He held up one finger. "For that night, the loser has to do anything the winner wants in bed." His gaze burned into hers, as if already he was picturing her naked and at his mercy.

She wet her lips. "I hope you've been taking your vitamins, then," she said. "You're going to need them."

"Are you two going to play cards or stand there making cow eyes at each other?" Leslie called.

With one last heated look, Garret turned toward her. "Deal 'em out, mates. We're ready."

The kitchen table had been extended to its full length and seven chairs arranged around it. Rachel found herself seated across from Garret, between Guy and Leslie. She stared at the first hand dealt her and suppressed a small thrill. Three aces winked back at her. Careful to show no expression, she discarded two cards and accepted two more. The fourth ace nestled in next to the other three. *So much for skill,* she thought.

She won the first hand neatly, lost the next, won the next. By the fourth hand, she had a feel for the game, and discovered a knack for reading her opponents' faces and judging their hands. Who knew all those hours of psychology classes would pay off at the poker table?

She accepted a beer from someone, and a sub sandwich from someone else. Players folded or left the table altogether and others took their places. Garret remained fixed in his seat across from her, focused on the cards with the intensity of a man determined not to lose.

Except he did lose. Often. His mood grew more grim with each hand, while Rachel was giddy with victory. "I'm so glad you invited me tonight," she said as she raked yet another stack of chips toward her. "I'm having so much fun."

"I thought you said she'd never played poker before," Tate said. "Turns out she's a regular Chris Ferguson."

"I had an excellent teacher," she said, smiling at Garret, who glared back at her.

"The Man Tamer is certainly taming the Wild Man at the poker table," Leslie said.

"Whatever you do," Guy said, "don't let her take up lacrosse."

"You never can tell," she said, her eyes locked to his, "I might be very good at handling a stick."

Hoots and laughter greeted this comment. Garret remained stone-faced, but Rachel thought she detected a hint of a smile in his eyes.

It was past two in the morning when they called it a night. Rachel cashed in her chips and accepted congratulations, then stood with Garret at the door to say goodbye to everyone.

When they were alone again, she turned and gave

him a long kiss. "You're not really upset that I won tonight, are you?" she asked.

"No, I'm a man who stands by his word. I'm ready to take my punishment." He slid his hands down to caress her bottom. "I might even be looking forward to it."

"But not tonight." She squirmed out of his grasp and surveyed the apartment. Beer bottles, chip bags and paper napkins littered the floor. Barney had his head in the trash can, eating something someone had discarded there. An overflowing ashtray sat on the counter and the sink was full of dirty dishes. "This place is a disaster area," she said.

"Don't worry about this." Garret put his hand on her shoulder and steered her toward the bedroom. "We have a bet to settle, remember?"

She shook her head. "The bet was we'd spend the night together. It's almost morning. Besides—" she turned toward him, stopping him in his tracks "—I want us both to be well rested when I claim my winnings."

"All right. Then let's call tonight a little preview." He grinned. "Your wish is my command."

Could she help it if she had an evil streak that she couldn't always succeed in quelling? Not to mention that this was a perfect time for a little man tamer training….

"Then I command you to help clean up this apartment," she said. She slipped from his arms and tossed a crumpled napkin his way.

The napkin hit him in the chest and fluttered to the floor. He stared at her. "It's half past two and you want to clean house?"

"Yes."

"But why? It'll all still be here in the morning."

She shook her head. "If you think I can sleep knowing all this is out here waiting, then you don't know women. Now get busy. We'll have this cleaned up in no time."

Muttering under his breath about "crazy women" and "obsessive-compulsive behavior" he began gathering up beer bottles and paper plates.

"Just promise me when it's time to claim your winnings, you're not going to expect me to spend the evening cleaning house."

"I don't know." She pretended to consider the idea. "A man with a vacuum cleaner in his hand can be very sexy."

"Pervert."

She laughed. "How about naked housework? That might be fun."

"If the two of us are naked in the same room, I can guarantee we won't be washing windows or scrubbing floors," he said. "Bet or no bet."

"You promised to do anything I wanted."

"In bed. I specifically said *anything the winner wants in bed.*"

"That could be anything, couldn't it?" She let her eyes linger on him, a mysterious smile on her lips. "Think of the possibilities." The idea was almost enough to make her skip cleaning and head straight to bed.

Almost, but not quite. After all, the Man Tamer had a reputation to maintain. And she'd been serious when she'd told him she wanted them to be well rested for what she had in mind.

8

Man-Taming Principles Three and Four: Distraction and Substitution.

Sometimes the best way to change bad behavior is to provide a little distraction or to substitute something else for the undesired behavior. Think about it. When you want to quit smoking, experts advise you give yourself something else to do with your hands. Dieters are told to take up a hobby or go for a walk to distract their minds from the urge to overeat. Distraction can work for man taming, too.

Let's say your man has a habit of telling off-color jokes in mixed company. Whenever you sense he's about to launch into one of these jokes, change the subject to another topic of conversation. If that doesn't work, you might have to resort to big-time distractions such as spilling your drink or stepping on his toe. Keep this up enough and he's gotten out of the habit of telling these jokes. (Of course, he may also think you're a horrible klutz, but such is the price we pay in the interest of bettering our lives.)

"You must be really gone on this guy if you agreed to look after his dog," Moira said as she followed Rachel up the stairs to Garret's apartment the following weekend. Rachel had promised to buy her dinner if she'd come with her to feed and walk Garret's beast. Moira had agreed not only for the free meal, but also for the fun of seeing her friend go one-on-one with what Rachel had claimed was "the most unruly dog in the world."

"It's only for two days," Rachel said as she inserted the key in the lock. "His normal pet sitter moved away and he didn't have anyone else."

"He could have hired another pet sitter. But I think it's sweet that—"

Frantic barking drowned out the rest of her words. Rachel shoved open the door and they were almost flattened by a furry brown whirling dervish. "Down, Barney! Get down!" Rachel shouted as she tried to fend off sloppy dog kisses. Barney's tail waved wildly, knocking over the umbrella stand by the door.

"He certainly seems to like you," Moira said, laughing. She only wished she had a camera. The calm, cool and collected Man Tamer being loved to distraction by this overgrown puppy.

The dog finally settled down enough for them to close the door and move all the way into the apartment. "You can tell a man lives here," Moira said, picking a shirt from the back of the sofa, then letting it drop. Clothes, shoes, newspapers and magazines were scattered around the living room. It looked just like Dave's apartment. "A woman would never leave town without cleaning up first."

"I think it's part of that whole in-your-face, 'this is me, take it or leave it' attitude men have," Rachel said.

She headed for the kitchen, Barney racing ahead, his toenails scrambling for purchase on the tile floor. "Maybe so," Moira said, following. "I guess that arrogance is one of those love it and hate it traits men have." She was doing a lot of loving and hating when it came to Dave these days. Another reason she'd come with Rachel tonight. She needed to talk about everything that was—and wasn't—happening in her love life. Rachel was so calm and logical, she could help Moira figure out what to do.

While Rachel poured kibble and added fresh water to the dog's bowl, Moira searched the cabinets.

"What are you looking for?" Rachel asked.

"Just seeing if Garret's kitchen is anything like David's." She pulled out a can of beer nuts and shook it. Maybe three nuts rattled around in the can. "The same," she said, and replaced the can in the cabinet.

"Please, if you're going to snoop, at least go for the good stuff," Rachel said.

Moira froze in the act of opening another cabinet and looked over her shoulder at her friend. "The good stuff?"

"You know—the medicine cabinet, the bedside table, the desk drawers. Everybody knows that's where you find all the good dirt on people."

"So are you planning to look in all those places in Garret's apartment?" Moira asked.

Rachel pressed her lips together and shook her head. "It wouldn't be right. I mean, he trusted me with the keys to the place for two days. I couldn't betray that trust."

"Maybe he knew he had nothing to hide," Moira said.

Rachel nodded. "Of course."

Moira turned to face her. "Aren't you a little bit curious?"

Rachel threw up her hands. "Duh! I'm *dying* of curiosity. Which is where *you* come in."

Moira laughed. "I get it. *You* can't search Garret's place because it wouldn't be honorable. But *I* could do it and tell you what I find."

"Only because you're my friend and you're looking out for my best interests," Rachel said. "Not because I put you up to it."

"Not at all. So where should we get started?"

"Bedroom." Rachel pointed toward a hallway. "Second door on the right."

The bedroom looked as if a tornado had recently whirled through, hurling bedcovers, books and clothes in heaps on the floor. The closet door stood open, dirty and clean garments mingling in a pile at the bottom. Moira pulled open the bedside table and inventoried the contents. "Box of condoms, tube of lube, two-month-old television guide, dog biscuit…ew, is that a mouthpiece?" She pointed to a twisted bit of plastic.

Rachel peered over her shoulder. "Looks like the kind the players wear during games."

"*Oooh,* here's something interesting!" Moira fished out a black lace thong. "Anyone you know?"

Rachel's face blushed bright pink. "That's mine," she said, snatching the underwear and shoving it back into the drawer. "Let's see what's in the bathroom."

The medicine cabinet was depressingly dull. "No pills, no potions, no illegal drugs," Moira said. "Just toothpaste, deodorant and shaving cream. And a bottle of aspirin."

Rachel grinned. "Is he a great guy or what?"

"You seem pretty happy we haven't found anything too interesting," Moira said as she followed Rachel into the living room and Garret's desk.

"Of course I'm happy. Every woman likes to have it confirmed that she's dating a nice guy."

"Uh-huh." Moira pulled out the desk drawer. "But he ought to have at least one bad habit or secret. If not, I'd be worried he was too perfect—and something sinister was hiding behind that great facade."

"You're much too cynical," Rachel said. "Now open the drawer."

The desk yielded several pictures of women, all of whom later showed up in what was clearly a family portrait. Moira also found two decks of cards, some Australian money, a lacrosse ball, bank statements and a copy of *Belinda* magazine.

"The latest issue," she said, handing the magazine to Rachel.

Rachel smoothed her hand over the cover, which featured a smiling local news anchor. "Do you think he bought it to read my column?"

"I doubt if he bought it to learn the 'Twelve Fashion Faux Pas to Avoid' or to 'Lose Ten Pounds in Ten Days on the Banana Split Diet.'"

Rachel smiled. "That's so sweet."

"You aren't worried all the stuff you write about Man Taming will scare him off?"

"This issue has been out a month. If he objected to anything I had to say, Garret would have told me by now. He doesn't strike me as the type to keep quiet when something upsets him." She slid the magazine back into the drawer. "Besides, why should he be upset? I'm not writing specifically about him."

"Dave would be upset," Moira said. Very early in their relationship, when he'd learned she was friends with Rachel, he'd made it clear he found the very idea of man taming offensive.

"That's Dave. Garret is different."

"He's a man, and aren't you the one always saying they have fragile egos?"

"Not Garret. He's not fragile at all. So how are things with you and Dave?"

Moira didn't miss the abrupt change of subject, but decided not to comment. She needed to talk to Rachel about Dave, and to figure out what to do next. "Did I tell you what happened when I invited him to dinner the other night?" she asked as the two women walked toward the kitchen. "He actually suggested I come to his place and cook instead. As if there was any way to put together a decent meal in his kitchen."

"So did you convince him to come over to your place?" Rachel stowed the dog food back under the sink.

"No. We ended up canceling." Moira slumped against the counter. "The sad thing is, he didn't even sound disappointed."

Rachel nodded. "Maybe he thought it's what you wanted. Guys are funny that way."

Moira shook her head, the knot that had rested in her

chest since last Friday evening tightening. "We've talked on the phone a few times since then and he acts as if everything is fine. But how can it be fine when he'd rather spend the evening with his big-screen TV than with me?"

Rachel came and put her arm around Moira. "No man in his right mind is going to choose TV over a woman like you. Which means Dave obviously isn't in his right mind."

"Yeah. So how do I bring him to his senses?"

Rachel considered the question. "Maybe it's time to do something shocking."

"Shocking? You mean, like stand naked in front of the television when he's trying to watch the game?" Moira had considered it, but the possibility that Dave might simply ask her to move out of the way had been too humiliating to face.

Rachel smiled. "I was thinking maybe it was time to have 'the talk' with David."

Moira's eyes widened. "'The talk'? Do you think he's ready?"

"More important, are *you* ready?"

Moira hesitated, then nodded. "I think so." She and Dave had been together over a year. It was high time they discussed where their relationship was really headed. "I've never had 'the talk' with a guy before. What do I say?"

"Tell him you love him, you want to spend time with him but you're not sure if he feels the same about you."

"And if he says he does?" That would be a good thing, right? But the idea didn't untie the knot in her stomach.

Rachel's expression was stern. "Then you have to ask him why he isn't showing you that. Tell him he needs to choose between you and the TV."

Moira swallowed hard. "But what if he chooses the TV?"

"Then you'll know." Rachel patted Moira's shoulder. "And you can get out there and find a man who will be the perfect man for you."

Did it make her pathetic—or just a woman truly in love—to admit that she wanted David to be that man? "The thing is," she said, trying to give voice to her fears, "what if the perfect man doesn't exist? I mean, David is a sports-crazy slob, but he's also funny and smart and hardworking and handsome and…and he can be really wonderful and loving."

"Do you think you're still in love with him?"

She nodded. "Yes." Hopelessly in love. Emphasis on hopeless.

Barney finished eating and wandered into the living room. Rachel and Moira followed. "What are you going to do?" Rachel asked.

Moira shook her head. "I don't know. Maybe counseling?"

"It's worth a try."

"Except I don't think I could convince David to go. He doesn't think anything is wrong with our relationship."

"Hmm. Could be a problem." Rachel set the umbrella stand upright and straightened its contents. "I still think it comes down to laying it on the line and seeing how he *really* feels." She gave Moira a sympathetic look. "Scary stuff, I know."

Moira hugged her arms across her chest. "You're right. I just have to find the right time to do it. It won't be this weekend anyway. He's in Portland on business."

"Really? That's where Garret is playing this weekend."

Moira watched Rachel straighten the pillows on the sofa. "How are things with you and Garret?" she asked.

Rachel smiled. "Good. I think he's really responding to my techniques." She picked a magazine off the floor and stacked it neatly on the coffee table, then gathered the newspapers and folded them.

"Really?" Moira looked around the apartment. She didn't see any signs of a transformation here. "In what ways?"

Rachel picked up the shirt and folded it. "He cleans up when I come over. And he wears blue shirts now because I told him they look good with his eyes."

"Because he wants you in the sack." Moira refrained from rolling her eyes. "Guys will do anything if they think it will lead to sex. When we were first dating, Dave actually told me he enjoyed going to the mall. That didn't last."

Rachel straightened a lamp shade. "No, I think he's really responding."

"So is the sex good?"

Rachel's smile widened. "The sex is fantastic."

"It must be, if you're willing to look after his dog while he's away."

"Oh, Barney isn't so bad." At the sound of his name, the dog loped over and leaned against her, almost knocking her over. "He's just a little…enthusiastic," she said, shoving him away.

"Uh-huh. So what else have you been doing? I mean, is it all lacrosse and sex?" Not that that sounded like such a bad agenda to her….

"No, we go out. I made dinner for him the other night and he taught me to play poker."

Moira laughed. "Poker! But you hate card games."

"This was fun. Garret has a bunch of friends who get together regularly to play and he wanted me to be a part of it." She looked smug. "And as a matter of fact, I'm pretty good at poker. I won."

Moira shook her head. "Uh-huh. Just who is training whom here?"

"What do you mean?"

"Well, he's got you cooking dinner for him, sleeping with him, looking after his dog and playing poker. You're even wearing his clothes."

Rachel looked down at the lacrosse jersey she wore over cut-off shorts. "Garret left this at my place. I didn't want to risk the dog messing up something of mine."

"Still, it sounds to me like you're the one making most of the changes in this relationship," Moira said.

"That's not true."

"I'm not saying it's a bad thing." Moira shrugged. "That's the way relationships work. Women always give up the most to make the man happy. But sometimes it sucks."

Rachel came over and put her hand on Moira's shoulder. "I'm sorry things aren't working out with you and Dave," she said. "You deserve someone who will treat you right—who won't make you do all the sacrificing in the relationship."

"Do you think you and Garret have that kind of relationship? I mean—is he 'the one' for you?"

Rachel looked away. "I think it's too soon to tell. But I do know things are going well. And I feel like I'm going to win my bet with Denton."

"So you'll have a great guy and your dream job. Congratulations." *I hate you.* Not really, but she wished she had that kind of luck herself.

"Things are going to work out for you," Rachel said. "If not with Dave, then with someone else."

"Right." Moira looked away. "Maybe I'll learn to play cards." If nothing else, it would keep her busy all those lonely Saturday nights in her future.

AFTER DEFEATING the Portland Lumberjacks 11-10, Garret and most of his teammates adjourned to Frankie's Sports Bar to celebrate. Most of the patrons probably thought the group of loud, large men were a bunch of buddies out for a Saturday night on the town. Professional indoor lacrosse was still an anonymous sport. The fame and fortune accorded basketball, football and baseball players wasn't something Garret and his buddies aspired to, anyway. They were content to work their day jobs and enjoy playing the game they loved on weekends.

Which didn't mean it wasn't flattering when a fan recognized them. "Hey, Wild Man Kelly!"

Smiling, Garret turned to greet the man who had hailed him. He had dark brown hair and wore a brown bomber jacket and looked vaguely familiar. "Great game tonight," the man said, coming over and offering his hand.

"Thanks, Mr.…?"

"David Brewer. Just call me Dave. We met at Denton Morrison's party last month."

"I remember now." He had a vague recollection of exchanging a few words with the bloke.

Dave squeezed in next to him at the bar. "Can I buy you a drink?"

"I'm good for now." Garret picked up his pint glass. "Let me buy you one."

The beer ordered, Dave turned the topic once more to lacrosse. "I saw the game tonight. The team looked sharp."

"Portland kept us on our toes." Garret sipped his beer. "Did you come all the way from Dallas to watch the game?"

"Nah. I was here on business, but when I saw you were in town I couldn't pass up the chance to go." He shrugged. "You know how it is in a town where you don't really know anyone. There's nothing much to do at night except watch TV in your room or hit the bars."

"Been there, done that," Garret acknowledged.

Bud joined them at the bar. "There's a crowd in here tonight," Bud said. He handed his empty glass to the bartender. "But the beer's good."

"Bud, this is Dave. He's from Dallas, too, up here on business."

The men shook hands. "You were at Denton's party, weren't you?" Bud said. "With that girl, Mariah?"

"Moira. That was me." Dave set his beer on the bar and looked around the crowded room before his gaze drifted back to Garret. "I saw something in the paper about you dating Rachel Westover, is that true?"

Garret nodded. "It's a sad thing when the public thinks a minor athlete's private life is worthy news."

"So what's up with all this man-taming stuff?" Bud took a handful of snack mix from a bowl on the bar.

"Rachel's column?" Garret snorted. "Just a gimmick to sell magazines." He hefted a new glass of beer. "Rachel's a great gal. She's not out to tame anyone." Unless he counted the way she'd tamed him in bed. Or brought out the *real* wild man. They had yet to have a free night for her to cash in her bet, but he had no doubt it would be an evening he wouldn't soon forget.

"Look at the way he's smiling," Bud said. He elbowed Garret in the ribs. "I'm thinking maybe the Man Tamer tried out some of her *techniques* on you and you liked them."

"I wouldn't know about that, mate. But whatever she's writing in that column, I know it wouldn't work on a real man."

"Damn straight," Dave said. "They're the ones that need to be tamed, not us."

"And since when do women want a domesticated pet for a partner?" Garret said, warming to the subject. "They might say they wish we were more refined, but who are they really attracted to? The rugged individual-ist, the bad boy, the rough-around-the-edges macho man."

"Women want a real man." Dave slammed down his empty glass.

"So she isn't going to tame you?" Bud said.

Garret shook his head. "No worries there, mate. Not gonna happen."

"Then why is the column so popular?" Bud asked. "I mean, is it all a big joke, or do women really believe that stuff?"

"They believe it." Dave's expression sobered. "I think Moira's even been trying out some of that man-taming shit on me."

Garret and Bud stared at him. "What's she been doing?" Garret asked.

"Oh, you know how women are—picking out my clothes for me, inviting me to dinner when she knows the hockey finals are being televised."

"But that's how women always act," Garret said. "I don't see what that has to do with man taming."

"Ah, that's what they want you to think. But this is more subtle. They're trying to get us to change—into something we never were. And if they were honest with themselves, they'd realize they never wanted that anyway." Dave shook his head. "The truth is, women are never happy with what they've got. There's no pleasing them."

"So we might as well give up and please ourselves," Bud said.

"Exactly!" Dave slapped him on the back. "That's what I intend to do."

"So I guess you've told Moira to give up her man-taming ways," Garret said.

"Not in so many words," Dave said. "But I think I've been pretty clear where I stand. She should love me the way I am. I'm not changing for anybody." He frowned into his half-empty glass.

"That's the way, mate." Garret patted his shoulder.

They drank in silence for a while, pondering the cunning and complexity of women.

"What does Moira think?" Bud asked after a while.

Dave looked more glum than ever. "She wasn't too happy, but she'll come around. After all, the two of us are good together."

Bud nodded. "Still, maybe it's a good idea to go along with women's ideas sometimes," he said. "I mean, they're different from us. They need different things."

Garret turned to his friend, surprised. He hadn't expected a man who was usually awkward and shy around women to have spent so much time contemplating them. "You've got it all wrong, mate," he said gently. "I'm telling you, women don't want a soft man. No matter what they say to the contrary."

"That's right," Dave said. "Women want a man who'll take charge. A man who'll stand up to them."

Bud nodded. "Maybe you're right." He drained the last of his beer and set aside the empty glass. "But if you are, why are the three of us spending Friday night in a bar with a bunch of guys instead of home in bed with a beautiful woman?"

Garret blinked. "We're out of town, that's why."

"Yeah, but if we were home, 'putting our foot down' about what we will or will not do, how likely is it we'd be snuggling with something warm and soft besides our pillow tonight?"

"A man needs time on his own," Dave said. He looked at Garret. "Right?"

Garret nodded. "We don't need a woman smothering us every minute."

"We need time to bond with the guys and watch the game," Dave said.

"To fart and not have to apologize for it," Garret added.

"To eat what we want to eat and wear what we want to wear," Dave said.

"To go home to an empty apartment," Bud added. He folded his arms across his chest and frowned at them.

They stared at him for a long moment, then Dave turned and signaled the bartender. "Three more beers," he said.

Garret nodded. This was how men handled such eternal questions as the meaning of women and love. Have another beer. Somewhere between a good buzz and getting pissed drunk, maybe enlightenment would come.

Then the trick was to remember it until morning.

9

Man-Taming Principle Five: Reprimanding Bad Behavior.

When positive reinforcement and the other gentler techniques fail to bring about the desired change, it's time to try a more negative approach. Not because you want to be cruel, but because sometimes, people behave poorly when they don't realize the impact their behavior has on others.

At its simplest level, this principle means that if your man is doing something you don't like, ask him to stop. You may have to ask more than once. Some men see this as nagging. I say that's merely passive-aggressive behavior on their part. They're the ones ignoring your request, so why make you out as the bad guy? So don't be afraid to use this principle, ladies. Sometimes standing up for ourselves is the very best way to get exactly what we want.

RACHEL COULDN'T REMEMBER when she'd been so nervous. She paced back and forth across the living room of her apartment, wobbling on the impossibly high heels of her boots and pausing every few steps to adjust the fishnet hose that kept creeping up her butt.

When she'd first decided to wear the dominatrix outfit to collect her "winnings" from Garret, she'd seen it as a lark. Something that would give them both a laugh. But what if he took it seriously? What if he expected her to use the whip that came as a prop with the outfit?

She eyed the miniature cat-o'-nine-tails. The thought of actually striking Garret with it made her shiver. No, that wasn't her idea of a turn-on. She only hoped he felt the same way.

Still, with men, you never knew. They might be the same species as women, but they were definitely a different animal….

The doorbell rang, surprising a squeal out of her. She teetered on her high heels, then checked the peephole, knowing before she did so that it was him. She was surprised to see him wearing a suit. And carrying flowers. Who was this guy and where had the pod people hidden her boyfriend?

She opened the door, shielding most of her body behind it. "Hi, there," she said, smiling. "You're awfully dressed up for an evening at home."

"I figured I might as well try to impress you with a suit." He stepped past her into the apartment. "With any luck, I won't have to keep the damn thing on long." He turned to present her the flowers and choked on the rest of his words. "Crikey!" He swore softly as he took in the thigh-high black boots, fishnet hose, black leather bustier and studded dog collar she wore.

"Do you like it?" she asked, realizing as she did so that that was about the most un-dominatrix-like statement she could have made.

He swallowed. "Let's just say I'm having some disturbingly perverted fantasies about now." He handed her the flowers. "For you, uh, mistress."

She took the flowers. "Why don't you open the wine while I put these in water?"

"Is that an order?" he teased, following her to the kitchen.

"Sure." She found a vase and arranged the flowers in it, wondering what to do next. She had only a vague idea of what she intended this evening.

He handed her the wine. "To you," he said, touching his glass to hers. He drank deeply, his eyes never leaving hers. She fought the urge to look away, to betray her nervousness.

"May I kiss you?" he asked.

She started to tell him he didn't need permission to kiss her, then realized he was getting into the act. Maybe even enjoying it. "You may," she said, taking his hand in hers and pulling him close.

His kiss said more about how much he was enjoying this game they were playing. How much he was enjoying *her*. From the first touch of his lips she forgot her nervousness and hesitation, forgot everything but the feel of his mouth on hers, the strength of his arms around her, the solid bulk of his chest pressed against her. As she wrapped her arms around his neck and shaped her body to his she realized she was caught between the desire for independence and control represented by her costume and the longing to be overtaken and cared for by this man.

She moved out of his arms, wanting more time to think. She led the way into the living room. "I haven't seen you since you got back from Portland," she said. "Let's talk for a little while."

"Thanks for looking after Barney," he said.

"Oh, he was no trouble." Except for being a little wild, the dog was really very sweet. And when else in her life had anyone looked at her with such pure adoration? "I'll bet he was glad to see you."

"He was. But he likes you, too." He set his wineglass on the coffee table and turned toward her, his expression serious. "Thanks for cleaning up my place, too. You didn't have to do that. In fact, I feel bad that you did."

"I didn't really clean, just straightened up a bit." She didn't mention going through his drawers and medicine cabinet. She still felt bad about that. What if she'd found something incriminating?

She had found the copy of *Belinda*. But that had been more flattering than damning. "How was Portland?" she asked. "I saw you won the game."

"Portland was great. Hey, I met a friend of yours in the bar afterward. Well, a friend of a friend, anyway. Dave Brewer."

"Moira's boyfriend," she said, surprised. "She told me he was there on business."

"Yeah, he came to watch the game and we met up afterward. Nice guy."

"Yeah." And Dave was a nice guy. Most of the time, except when he was making Moira so unhappy.

He picked up his wineglass again and drank. "Have you talked to Denton lately?"

"No. Have you?"

"Yeah, he called me into his office last week. He's still keen for us to make some public appearances together."

She shrugged. "I don't really mind if you don't." She smiled. "Our relationship isn't exactly secret, what with all the items Denton's planted in the gossip columns."

"Hmm." He nodded, a mischievous look flooding his eyes as he scanned her costume. "Maybe we should have you dress like this." He touched her thigh where the boot ended and the fishnet began. "I bet he'd love that—you as a *real* man tamer, whip and all."

She shook her head, thoroughly creeped out by the idea. "I'd be afraid Denton might love it *too* much. The man is a little odd when it comes to women."

"I see what you mean. All those young girls." He laughed. "Don't take this wrong, but when I first saw the two of you together, at his party, I was worried you might be one of his conquests."

She shuddered. "Yuck. Never. Besides, I'm probably not young enough for him."

"Thank God for that."

She set aside her empty glass. "If nothing else, I'd be afraid Denton would want to start running a picture of me dressed like this at the top of my column." It would be just like him to think something like that was hip.

"Speaking of your column, I read last month's," Garret said. "The one about distracting from bad behavior."

She nibbled her lower lip. "You did?"

"Yeah, I did. Great stuff, that. Very well written and entertaining. I suppose it could even work with some people."

Relief flooded her at his praise, along with amusement at his final qualifier. "But it wouldn't work on you," she said.

He laughed. "Nah. But why would you want to change anything about me?"

Only for a chance at my dream job, she thought. And *change* was really too strong a word. She liked Garret the way he was, he only needed a little... refining.

"So, mistress, what do you have planned for this evening?" he asked.

She thought of the column she'd written that morning, about reprimanding bad behavior. Not that Garret had been bad, but he *had* lost the bet they'd made at the poker party. And that deserved some sort of penalty. And since she was wearing a dominatrix costume and he'd already admitted that turned him on...

She stood, looming over him in the five-inch heels. "Take off your clothes," she said, keeping her voice stern.

"Yes, ma'am." He stood and began loosening his tie.

She sat back on the sofa, facing him. Legs crossed, she jiggled her foot, impatient. "Stand on the coffee table, where I can see you," she commanded. Fortunately, it was a solid wood table, strong enough to support his weight.

He didn't hesitate, but stepped up onto the table and continued to strip. She had to admit she was getting turned on, watching him. She let her gaze roam over his body, lingering on the muscled ridges of his abdomen, the hard planes of his thighs, the growing erection rising from the thick thatch of black hair at his crotch. She squeezed her legs tighter together.

"Like what you see?" Garret asked.

"Mmm." She pointed to the clothes scattered around the table. "Pick those up and fold them neatly."

"You have a thing for neatness, don't you?" he said as he stooped to pick up his shirt.

She shifted on the sofa. "There's nothing wrong with wanting things tidy."

"I never said there was." He rolled his socks into a ball and set them atop the folded pants, shirts and shorts. "What now…mistress?"

A real dominatrix probably would have disciplined him for the borderline insolence in his voice, but Rachel was more amused than angry. She liked that he continued to assert his masculinity even as he played the submissive—that maybe he was as uncertain of how far they should go with this game as she was.

What now? She wanted more than compliance from him. She wanted…connection. "Did you really like my column?" she asked.

"I think you're a very good writer," he said. "I can't say it's something I'd have ever picked up if I didn't know you, but it kept me reading. I'd like to read more."

Praise as an aphrodisiac was a new experience for her. Perhaps it was his sincerity—or the fact that he was naked—that turned her on so, but the effect was electric.

Every nerve ending buzzed with repressed longing as she took his hand and pulled him toward the bedroom.

"I want you to undress me," she said, stopping at the foot of the bed.

He reached for the bustier and began rapidly undoing the hooks. She put up her hand to stop him. "Slowly."

"Sorry," he mumbled, fumbling with another hook. "I can't help myself." He released the last hook and the garment parted. She shrugged her shoulders and let it fall to the floor. She sat on the end of the bed and extended one leg so that he could help her remove the boot.

He took his time taking off the boots, tugging them oh-so-slowly down her thighs and along her calves. The supple leather brushed against her skin and his fingers trailed after. He kept his gaze locked to hers, both his looks and his gestures teasing her, heightening her anticipation.

Boots off, he reached up and slid his fingers beneath the waistband of the fishnet tights. He stripped her underwear off with the tights, shoving them to her ankles. She stood again and stepped out of the hose, and faced him once more, naked.

He stared at her, his hands clenching and unclenching. "It's damned hard to keep my hands off you when you're naked."

"What are we going to do about that?" she teased. Not that him touching her was such a bad idea....

"Maybe you need to tie me up."

His words sent a jolt of unexpected heat through her. "Would you like that?" she asked.

His gaze flickered away, then back to her. He swallowed. "Would you?"

The hesitation beneath his eagerness stirred her. Perhaps he was caught, too, torn between a masculine instinct for control and the attraction of surrender. "Maybe I would."

She led him to the bed and he lay back. Just the sight of him there, waiting for her to make the next move, made her heart race and her nipples tighten. She bound his hands and feet with scarves she took from her closet, taking her time, enjoying the feel of the cool silk sliding through her hands, contrasted to the heat of his skin. She kept her gaze on him as she worked, watching him watch her. "You're not nervous?" she asked.

"Should I be? Are you going to hurt me?"

She picked up the whip and trailed it across her palm. "I could."

"I don't believe you would."

She knelt beside him and trailed the ends of the whip across his chest, the feathery touch teasing his nipples. She watched the muscles of his stomach contract as she tickled him with the knotted ends of the leather strands. By the time she let the ends of the whip wrap around his erect penis they were both breathing hard.

There was something to be said for having him at her mercy like this. Though he wasn't entirely helpless. She had no doubt if he wanted he could break the bonds without too much trouble. So the fact that he allowed himself to be subject to her whim moved her in a way that went beyond desire.

She trailed the whip along his thighs, down his

calves, then tossed it aside and straddled him. His gaze remained locked to hers, burning into her. He was very erect, straining toward her. She stroked his penis with one finger, the contrast of silken, heated flesh over his rock-hard erection sending a rush of liquid warmth between her legs.

He made a low, growling noise in his throat. She jerked back her hand. "Is something wrong?"

"Only that you're driving me crazy."

"Maybe you'd like me to stop." She climbed off him and walked to the head of the bed to stand beside him.

"Don't stop," he growled. He strained at his bindings. "Don't you dare stop."

Without a word, she turned and left the room. She thought he might protest, or call after her, but he remained silent. The man had patience, she had to hand it to him. While she was growing more impatient by the minute.

She collected a few things from the kitchen, then returned to the bedroom. He raised his head and eyed the items in her hand. "Hungry?" he asked.

"I thought you might be." She opened a jar of hot fudge sauce and dipped her finger in, then offered it to him.

The feel of his tongue wrapped around her finger, the suction of his mouth and velvety caress of his lips made her weak at the knees. She sat down and withdrew her hand from him. "Good," he said. His grin was positively wicked. "Maybe you'd like to try a chocolate-dipped cock."

She laughed, but the idea inspired her. Feeling a little self-conscious, she dipped out another fingerful of fudge and smeared it across her nipples. The topping was cold, and her nipples tightened in response. "Oops!" she said, setting the jar on the nightstand. "I seemed to have spilled some. Maybe you could help clean it up?"

"My pleasure." He strained toward her.

She helped him out by leaning toward him. The first touch of his mouth to her breast set up an insistent throbbing between her legs. His tongue and lips stroked relentlessly, sucking and licking, removing every drop of chocolate from first one breast, then the other. She moaned, leaning into him, every nerve on edge with wanting him, sure one touch to her clit would send her over the edge.

He lay back and smiled at her. "I wish you could see yourself now," he said. "Your breasts all glistening wet, your nipples two hard points." He shifted his gaze downward, toward her mons. "Why don't you climb back on me? Maybe you could spill some fudge down there, too."

The thought of him showing the same attention to her clit that he'd just shown her breasts was almost enough to make her climax right then and there. Moving carefully, she straddled him once more, every brush of skin on skin reminding her of how much she wanted him inside her.

She moved closer, sliding her mons the length of his erection, watching his eyes glaze over with need. Suddenly even this contact wasn't enough. She reached up and untied the scarf that bound his hands.

"What are you doing?" he asked.

"I want to feel your arms around me." She reached

back and unbound his feet, as well, then laid her head on his chest. "Now make love to me. Make me feel as incredible as I know you can."

His arms embraced her, and he kissed the top of her head, then rolled them onto their sides and kissed her eyes, her cheeks, her lips. He cupped her breast in one hand as if measuring the fullness, while she reached around to run her hands down his back, feeling his muscles bunch with each movement.

He bent and drew her nipple into his mouth with gentle suction, the swiftness of the movement catching her by surprise. She arched against him, eyes closed, every sense focused on the feel of his mouth against that sensitive tip.

She sighed when he released her, then drew a sharp breath in as he moved slowly down her body, painting her skin with kisses. The contrast of coolness and warmth, of wet and dry, of the pressure of his hands and the weight of his mouth on her assaulted her senses, making her dizzy, building the ache inside her.

He traced the indentation of her navel, then slid to her clit, his mouth covering her. She thrust against him, hands clutching at the sheets, frustration growing almost past bearing. "Your wish is my command, mistress," he said, answering her silent plea.

He launched a skilled assault on her clit, his tongue stroking, plunging into her then retreating, keeping up a steady onslaught of sensation. Her climax was sudden and forceful, washing over her in waves, the bed knocking against the wall with the force of her thrusts toward him.

He rose and moved quickly to sheath himself in a condom and enter her, then rolled over so that she was on top, her legs on either side of his hips, her hands braced against his chest.

She smiled down on him, watching his eyes as she oh-so-slowly slid the length of his shaft, then descended again, quicker this time. She thrust herself against him, burying him as deeply as possible, then drew back once more, wanting to feel every inch of him, to savor her body's response to him inside her.

He rested his hands lightly on her hips, allowing her to call all the shots. He was stronger than her, more powerful. He could have taken his pleasure from her any way he wished. But for now at least, he was willing to surrender control. Was there any greater strength than this?

She felt the powerful surge of his climax, his muscles tensing, pelvis thrusting. She rested her palms flat against his chest and rode the wave of his release, rising up with each hard thrust before finally sinking down onto him and rolling off and onto her side.

"I guess you've figured out I'd make a lousy dominatrix," she said.

He laughed. "But you looked great in the costume."

"I suppose that counts for something."

He caressed her shoulder. "I don't really see you as a submissive, either," he said. "Unless there's some hidden side to you I haven't yet seen."

She made a face. "No. I'm not the submissive type." She turned toward him, and reached up to stroke his face. "This is how I like things. Give and take on both sides. No one person gets to have all the fun."

"Strong words from a man tamer." He captured her hand in his and kissed the tips of her fingers. "I think you're right."

"Strong words from a wild man."

He lay back once more, still holding her hand in his. "Don't tell Denton. He'd never believe it."

"Like I said before, the man has some strange ideas."

"Pairing the two of us was one of his better ones, I'd say."

"Yeah. It was." She felt only a twinge of guilt at the words. What did it matter how she and Garret came to be a couple, as long as they were? What he didn't know would never hurt him. All she needed was to convince Denton that she'd won their little bet and she and Garret could continue as if nothing had ever happened. She'd have her television show, and a great guy, and life would be perfect.

10

Man-Taming Principle Six: Withhold Affection. Sometimes drastic measures are required to get a man's attention and let him know you're serious about your desire for him to change a behavior that is negatively impacting your relationship. One way to wake up a man to the consequences of his action is to withhold affection.

I'm not only talking about withholding sex, though that may very well come into play. But this principle works just as well in nonsexual relationships. Refuse the warmth, smiles and interaction—the pleasure of your company if you will—until the offender changes his ways.

Caution: this approach is not to be used lightly or maliciously. It's a drastic measure for when nothing else works, but you still feel there's hope for change.

GARRET FIRED A SHOT toward the net, sailing the ball neatly through the goaltender's legs and scoring a goal.

Or it would have been a score during a game. Since this was a practice, the goaltender lobbed the ball back into play and Garret and the rest of the offense ran off the court while the defensive players took their places.

"What's Denton Morrison doing here?" Bud asked as he and Garret headed for the water cooler.

Garret followed Bud's gaze to the sidelines, where the team owner stood, alone, watching the defense drill. Denton was a familiar face at games, but Garret couldn't remember him ever showing up at practice before. He shrugged. "Beats me. A bloke with that much money probably doesn't need a reason."

The whistle blew, summoning the offensive players back into position. As Garret headed for the court, he heard someone call his name. "Kelly!"

He looked up and saw Denton waving him over.

"What's up?" he asked as he approached the owner.

"Meet me in the bar when you're done here. We need to talk."

Garret suppressed a groan and nodded. "Sure." In his experience, Denton would do most of the talking, and Garret wouldn't much like what he had to say. The perks of being the big boss.

An hour later, freshly showered and looking forward to a cold beer, Garret found Denton in the arena bar. The place was supposed to be closed but he wasn't surprised that Denton had found a bartender somewhere, who obligingly opened a bottle of Foster's before Garret even asked.

"What brings you to slum with the working stiffs?" Garret asked as he sipped the beer.

"You looked good out there," Denton said. He sipped a scotch. "Five goals and two assists last game. Impressive."

Garret nodded in acknowledgment. "I try to do my part."

"You also haven't had a penalty in three games. Unheard of for the Wild Man."

"They've been good clean games. As a team we're focused on lessening our penalty kill situations."

Denton's eyes met his, a cool gray assessment. "The fans expect to see the Wild Man playing hard and getting in the box."

"Fans wants us to win games, too."

"You can do both. You've done it before."

Garret pushed aside the empty beer glass and declined the bartender's offer of another. "You can't sit there and tell me to play dirty."

"I'm not telling you to play dirty. Just play like the Wild Man." He frowned. "And what's with the suit?"

Garret looked down at his double-breasted navy suit jacket. "You don't like it?" He smoothed the lapels. "Rachel picked it out."

Denton's scowl deepened. "That's another thing. You're seeing too much of her."

Garret clenched his fists, anger flaring, but kept his voice under control. "You're the one who wanted us to hang out together—to play up the Man Tamer and Wild Man thing."

"How can you be a Wild Man when you're tied to one woman? Especially one known as the Man Tamer?" Denton finished off his drink and ordered another. "It's time for you to get out more. Be seen with some beautiful models or dancers or something."

Garret leaned closer, his bulk looming over the

smaller man. "You can't tell me how to live my private life."

Denton didn't flinch. "I hired you to be the public face of the team."

"Which means I'll do commercials. Pose for ads, make appearances and do charity work. You can't dictate who I date and don't date."

Denton studied Garret, a calculating look in his eyes. "Just how serious is it with you and Rachel?" he asked after a moment.

"None of your business."

"That tells me it is either serious and you don't want me to know, or it's serious and you're not yet ready to admit it to yourself."

Garret said nothing. He was ten seconds away from turning around and walking out of there. It was either that or punch Denton in the mouth, and he had more sense than to let his temper get him into that kind of trouble.

Denton shook his head. "You're making a mistake getting involved with Rachel," he said. "She's the type of woman who takes things seriously. All that man-taming claptrap she writes about is nothing more than propaganda to teach other women how to reel a man in. They'll promise you happiness, lead you to the altar, then make you miserable, suck you dry and cut you loose to move on to the next victim."

"Since when are you an expert on male-female relationships?" Garret asked.

"Since my third divorce. Trust me, what you want is a pretty piece of arm candy to provide a little fun and companionship. All the benefits without the commitment."

"I prefer women I might actually have something in common with," Garret said.

Denton snorted. "You think men and women ever have anything in common? If you do, you're fooling yourself." He slid off the bar stool, took out a money clip and peeled off two twenties for the bartender. "Take my advice and stay single as long as you can. You'll be a lot happier for it." He put his hand on Garret's shoulder. "And give me a little more Wild Man—on and off the courts. It's what the fans want and it's what I want."

Not waiting for an answer, he strolled out of the bar, leaving Garret feeling a little dizzy from the onslaught of *advice.* He sat at the bar again.

"Something else for you, sir?" the bartender asked.

"Yeah. Another Foster's." Though it would probably take more than one more beer before much of his conversation with Denton made sense.

The man had a twisted view of women, though maybe three divorces would do that to any guy. Garret sipped his beer and replayed Denton's words in his head. *She's the type of woman who takes things seriously.* He wouldn't argue with that assessment. Rachel did approach most things, whether it was a poker game or sex, with a certain gravity. But that was part of her charm. She was the kind of woman a man could trust not to take him too much for granted. After so many years on his own, it was good to know that what he was doing right now, what he had to say and what was going on in his life was important to someone else.

And he felt the same way about her. Did that mean he

was in love? The idea had been lingering at the edge of his consciousness for weeks now but it had taken his confrontation with Denton to get it out in the open. It was an idea he could get used to, though he preferred to let it sit there awhile before he risked saying anything to Rachel.

Was she in love with him? If love meant picking out a man's clothes, cleaning his apartment, smiling in her sleep as she lay naked next to him and putting up with a big hairy dog she didn't really like—then he'd say she was in love.

The idea gave him a rush akin to firing in a championship-winning goal. He set the half-full beer bottle carefully on the bar and took a deep breath, trying to slow his heart. "Steady, mate," he told himself. "No sense doing anything rash." He'd keep this to himself for a while until he had a game plan fixed in his head. Then he could move forward, knowing what both his offense and his defense would be.

"Go, Garret! Go, go, go. Yes!" Rachel jumped up and punched her fist in the air as Garret scored yet another goal for the Devils. Around her the crowd erupted in a deafening roar as an Arizona Sting player took possession of the ball and raced toward the opposite end of the arena. Dave whistled loudly and cheered as well, while Moira looked on, amused.

When they sat again, Moira nudged Rachel. "I never thought I'd see the day when you were this into a sport," she said.

"It's a lot more interesting when you understand

what's going on. Oooh!" She winced as a Devils player took a hit to the head. "Hey, Ref, are you blind?" she called.

"Hey, I'm not knocking it," Moira said. "I think it's fun. It's just a side of you I've never seen before."

The buzzer sounded, ending the third quarter. Dave stood and stretched. "I'm going for a hot dog," he said. "Y'all want anything?"

"I'm okay," Moira said.

"No thanks," Rachel said. She watched Dave head up the aisle, then turned to Moira. "So how are things going with you two?"

Moira shrugged. "Not a lot has changed. I mean, we're still together, but he's still glued to the TV most nights and…" She frowned.

"What is it?" Rachel prompted.

"I don't know. It's almost as if he's distancing himself from me on purpose. I mean, he's always been sports crazy, but I'm beginning to wonder if it's just an excuse not to be closer to me."

"Maybe he's afraid."

"Of what? That we might have an actual conversation?"

"Maybe his feelings for you are more intense than any he's had for any other woman and that's freaking him out a little," Rachel said. "When that happens, sometimes people pull back. It's a kind of self-defense."

Moira looked skeptical. "I don't know. I almost get the feeling Dave just doesn't trust me. Sometimes when we're talking, he has this expression on his face…like he's suspicious."

"Why wouldn't he trust you? It's probably just the whole fear-of-commitment thing."

"So what am I supposed to do to get past that?"

"Are you still using the techniques?"

Moira's gaze shifted to the court, where a dozen dancers in spandex suits were performing to a hip-hop beat. "Some of them. Sometimes."

"Maybe it's time to get drastic," Rachel said.

Moira looked at her. "Such as?"

"Withholding affection? Or punishment." Rachel named steps six and seven of her man-taming principles.

Moira shook her head. "I couldn't do that."

"I'm not talking about anything hostile. Tell him you want to take a break from each other. See what kind of reaction you get."

"No. That's too drastic."

"If he really loves you, it could be the wake-up call he needs."

"Or it could be the end. Call me a coward, but I'm not ready for that."

Rachel nodded. "When you're ready, then. And you know I'm here for you to vent."

"Thanks." Moira managed a weak smile. "Speaking of relationships, how are things with you and Garret? You two have been seeing each other for quite a while now."

"Four months, one week and three days." Rachel laughed. She'd been seeing Garret longer than any man she'd dated in the past five years. "It's going great."

"So is it serious?" Moira asked.

"I'm not sure." Rachel hesitated, then added, "I like him a lot."

"Like-like? Or like-love?"

What did it mean that her stomach fluttered like crazy at the mere mention of the word? "I don't know. Maybe love. But I'm scared I'll jinx it."

"What about your bet?"

Her expression brightened. "I have *so* won the bet. I just have to get Denton to admit it."

"And he won't?"

"He's avoiding me." Denton had failed to return any of her e-mails or phone calls and attempts to see him at his office had been met with stonewalling from his secretary.

"What proof do you have that the Wild Man is tamed?" Moira asked.

"He's dressing better since we've met." Partly because Rachel had bought him new clothes. "He keeps his apartment neater, at least when I'm there." He'd learned if he didn't, she'd insist on cleaning when she came over, which drove him nuts. "He actually signed Barney up for obedience training, *and* he hasn't been in the penalty box in four weeks."

"That's because of you?"

"Well, no. But it *is* proof that the Wild Man isn't so wild anymore. And I'll take credit for that if it will get me the television show."

Moira leaned closer and lowered her voice. "Does Garret know about the bet?"

"No. And don't you dare say a word to him."

Moira frowned. "You think he'd be upset if he knew?"

Of course he would be upset. Which is why Rachel was determined he never find out. "He knows about my column," she said. "He's even read it."

"And?"

"And he thinks it's cool. He actually said I was a very talented writer." She still felt ten feet tall, remembering his praise.

"I wonder if he'll feel the same way when you're on television where everyone can see you."

Rachel groaned. "According to Rhonda, I'm going to ruin her life by making a fool of myself in public, but Garret isn't like that. I think he'll be truly happy for me."

Loud cheers as the team jogged onto the court for the final quarter of play drowned out any further attempt at conversation. Dave returned with an extra-long hot dog and beer, and before he was settled in his seat the Devils scored another goal.

They ended up winning the game, 14-9, sealing a berth in the playoffs. As the players exchanged fist bumps with the opposing team, Rachel crowded to the rail at the side of the arena. Garret spotted her and came over.

She greeted him with a hug and a kiss on his beard-stubbled cheek. "Congratulations," she said.

"Thanks. Hey, Dave. Hey, Moira," He greeted Rachel's two companions. "Let me get cleaned up and we'll all go to eat or something."

"Hey, that would be—"

Moira elbowed Dave. "We'll take a rain check," she said. "You two have fun."

Rachel thought Dave wanted to protest, but Moira had hold of his arm and was pulling him toward the exit. For a small woman, she was pretty strong. Rachel had a feeling things would eventually work out for her friend and Dave. In her experience, a man in love was no match for a determined woman.

Garret turned to her. "Alone at last," he said, grinning. "Where do you want to go for dinner?"

"Why don't we pick up some burgers and go back to my place?" she said. They'd both been so busy lately they hadn't spent many quiet evenings at home.

"It'll have to be my place," he said. "Barney will want out, plus I need to dump off my gear."

"Okay."

"You don't mind?"

She shook her head. "I don't." It wouldn't be as neat as her place, but Garret was more sloppy than out-and-out dirty. And as she'd told Moira, he was good about picking up for her.

She waited for him outside the locker room. When he joined her he was freshly shaved and showered, dressed in jeans, the new polo shirt she'd picked out for him and a sport coat. "Mmm, you smell nice," she said, burying her nose in his neck and rubbing his smooth cheek.

"It's true what they say about this cologne then," he said. "I had to fight off three women on my way out."

She laughed and swatted at him. "Liar."

"All right then, only one woman. And I'm not exactly fighting hard." He pulled her closer.

She reluctantly shoved him away. "Come on. I'm hungry."

They picked up burgers at a drive-thru—including one for Barney—then headed for Garret's apartment, where Rachel laid out the food and poured drinks while he took the dog for a run around the block.

While they ate they discussed the game and Garret's travel schedule for the playoffs. Then he said, "I had an interesting conversation with Denton yesterday after practice," he said as he sat across from her at the kitchen table.

"Oh?" At least their boss was speaking with *someone.* "What did he have to say?"

He fed a French fry to the dog, who had devoured his burger in three bites. "He thinks I should stop seeing you."

She stared at him, heart pounding. Her vision went gray and she struggled to take a breath. "What?" she gasped.

"He thinks having a steady girlfriend, especially one known as the Man Tamer, is bad for my image."

"What do *you* think?"

"I told him to stuff it." He swept a French fry through a pool of ketchup and grinned. "Not in those exact words, but the message was the same."

"The nerve of that man." She ground her teeth together, thinking of fifty names she'd like to hurl at Denton—none of them flattering. Obviously he realized he'd lost their bet and was trying to sabotage her.

Garret pushed back his chair and patted his lap. "Come over here and kiss me, and I'll make you forget all about Denton what's-his-name."

She drank the last of her diet Coke, then came around the table and straddled him, letting him pull her onto his lap. They kissed with the warmth and familiarity of experienced lovers, yet the act had lost none of its passion. She nibbled gently at his lower lip, then traced the slick surface of his teeth with her tongue, tasting salt and sweetness, the heat between them building slowly.

He slanted his mouth more firmly against hers, teasing her with the dart-and-retreat of his tongue, his breath warm against her cheek.

He smoothed his hand down her back, then grasped her bottom and brought her more firmly against his erection. She ground against him, smiling at his groan of pleasure. He kissed the soft underside of her neck and she arched to him, still smiling, her happiness almost too great to contain. There was such joy in being with a man who knew how you liked to be touched and what sensations most pleased you. And such power in knowing the same things about him.

He slid his hand beneath her shirt and released the front clasp of her bra, then began fondling her breasts. He rolled the nipples between his thumb and forefinger, every movement adding to the heavy heat between her legs.

She squirmed against him and he put a hand on her thigh, keeping her still. "I've got you now," he growled. "Right where I want you."

"And where is that?" She pressed her pelvis against him, sliding up and down the length of his hard cock.

"How about right…here." He slid his hand up her thigh, beneath her skirt to the edge of her underwear. He stroked across her crotch, teasing her through the thin silk of her panties. Then he slid one finger beneath the elastic and into her. "Mmm, you're wet," he said, nuzzling her neck. "And tight."

Speech deserted her as his finger slid out of her

vagina and up across her clit. She could only whimper and dig her fingers into his shoulders as he increased the pace of his stroking.

He bent his head and drew one nipple into his mouth, rubbing the fabric of her shirt across the sensitive tip with his tongue. "That's…good," she moaned, her thighs clamped tight around him.

He raised his head and looked at her. "I love watching you when you're so turned on," he said.

"You just like watching," she teased.

He smiled. "I do at that."

She reached between them and unbuttoned his jeans, then grasped the zipper and lowered it. He grunted as her knuckles brushed across his erection. "Careful there," he said.

"Oh, I'll be careful." She shifted to create more space between them and wrapped her fingers around his shaft. His eyes lost focus as she began to stroke.

"Do you think…we should go…bedroom?" he said.

"Why? Are you uncomfortable?"

He shook his head. "You?"

She settled herself more snugly against him, the silk of her underwear against the heated flesh of his penis. "No. I'm not uncomfortable at all." Though the tension within her was building toward discomfort, a discomfort he could soon relieve.

He tugged at the waistband of her skirt. "I think you'd be more comfortable if you were naked," he said.

"You're probably right." She pulled her shirt over her head and tossed it aside, along with her bra, then, keeping one hand on his shoulder to balance herself, slid off his lap and stripped off her skirt and underwear. "Your turn," she said.

He skimmed off pants, boxers and shirt in record time, then pulled her into his arms and kissed her long and slow, their bodies shaped to one another. One hand caressed her bottom while the other cradled her shoulder, a gentle, almost protective posture that reminded her again of how glad she was to be with him.

When he broke the kiss she smiled up at him, then planted her hands on his shoulders and pushed him back toward the chair. "Where were we?" she asked.

He helped her straddle him again, this time poised with the head of his penis at the entrance to her vagina. "Somewhere along in here?"

They'd dispensed with condoms weeks ago, after they each were confident the other was healthy and she'd reassured him she was on the pill. So there was nothing to stop her now from sliding onto him. Guided by his hands on her hips, she thrust hard against him, leaning back to make the fullest contact. He took advantage of this posture to take her breast in his mouth once more, the feel of his mouth on her and his erection in her making her feel as if she was burning from the inside out, literally glowing with desire.

She stood on tiptoe and moved over him, her strokes slow, then swifter. He thrust up to meet her, the legs of the chair rising up with each stroke, then coming down hard. Thump, thump, thump! A drumbeat marking the rhythm of their passion. She smiled as she became aware of the sound, then it was drowned out by the thrumming of blood in her veins and her labored breathing as she approached her climax.

She squeezed her thighs around him, every muscle tensed to the point of trembling. His grip on her tightened and his voice was a low rasp. "Come on. You're almost there. Let me hear you come."

He reached up and tweaked her nipple and she went off like a rocket, screaming his name as he bucked against her, his own cries joining hers as he climaxed, also. They moved through the aftershocks, clinging to each other tightly, then collapsed against each other, eyes closed, waiting for their hearts to slow and breathing to return to normal.

She didn't know how much time passed before she opened her eyes, but when she did, she let out a laugh.

"What is it?" Garret asked, raising his head.

"Look!" She pointed to the chair and he joined her in laughing. They were now six feet from the table.

"I guess you could say we were moved by passion," he said.

She punched his shoulder, still laughing. "Where's Barney?" she asked, looking around. The dog's usual spot beside the table was vacant.

"You probably scared him away with all that hollering," Garret said.

"I wasn't singing a solo." She hugged him tightly. "You do make me feel the most wonderful things," she said.

"Ditto." He wrapped his arms around her and rested his chin on her shoulder. "And I have a confession to make."

Her heart skipped a beat. "What's that?"

"If anyone could tame this Wild Man, I'd have to say

it was you. I can't say I've ever been quite so...comfortable with anyone before."

"Comfortable?" She suppressed her disappointment at the word. Comfortable was for old shoes, faded chairs and worn jeans. Then again, she reminded herself, men delighted in such things.

"You know. At ease. Right." He raised his head and looked at her, his gaze assessing, like a detective searching for clues. "If you're not careful, you'll have me falling in love with you."

She swallowed the knot of happy tears that clogged her throat. "Would that be such a bad thing?"

He shook his head slowly. "No-o-o. Not such a bad thing at all."

They embraced again, and she couldn't stop smiling. As declarations went, it wasn't earth-shattering. But there was so much feeling behind his words, she had little doubt of the meaning there. What they had together was truly special, and she would fight with everything she had to keep Denton or anyone else from screwing it up.

11

Man-Taming Principle Seven: Punish Bad Behavior.

The very idea of punishment makes many people queasy. And this Man-Taming principle is not for the faint of heart. But used under the right circumstances, and in small doses, it can be quite an effective tool.

Mind you, I'm not referring to physical punishment. No whips and chains involved (though if you want to indulge in that sort of thing on your own time, who am I to judge?) No, I'm talking about withholding of privileges and even the occasional silent treatment. If your man isn't getting the message any other way, punishment may be the one method that gets his attention.

"I KNOW HE'S IN HIS OFFICE, Karen. I saw him go in." Rachel faced Denton's secretary across the black-laminate credenza outside the media mogul's office. "He's going to have to speak with me sooner or later."

"Mr. Morrison is very busy right now," Karen said, avoiding Rachel's eyes. "If you'd care to make an appointment he could probably see you sometime next month."

Rachel could think of half a dozen angry responses to this lame offer—none of which would get her in to see Denton. So she silently fumed and agreed to make an appointment for late May. Not that she had any intention of waiting that long to make her boss pay up on their bet.

She left the office and started for the elevator, but stopped short beside a bench across from the alcove. She glanced back at Denton's office. He'd have to leave sooner or later, and though spending the afternoon stalking him wasn't her idea of fun, this was definitely for a good cause.

Ninety minutes later her patience paid off when Denton emerged from his office and headed for the elevator. Rachel waited until the doors opened, then sprinted from her alcove and joined him in the car. "Hello, Denton," she said. "I'm so glad to see you."

"I don't have time to talk now, Rachel," he said, eyeing the panel of buttons as if contemplating making his escape on an upcoming floor.

Rachel stepped in front of the panel and smiled at him. "This won't take long. I just wanted to ask when I could start my new television show in that afternoon time slot on KTXK."

"What television show?" he asked, his expression bland. The man was probably a good poker player.

"The one you promised me if I won our bet to tame Wild Man Kelly."

"That?" Denton laughed. "You haven't tamed the Wild Man."

"I have and you know it."

"I know no such thing."

She struggled to keep her temper in check. After all, she'd come prepared to convince him. "The Wild Man is tamed. Ask anyone who knows him and they'll agree. He's dressing much better these days, and keeping his apartment neater. He's not out partying every night anymore. I know, because he's with me." She smiled in triumph. "You could even say the fact that he and I have dated steadily for over four months is proof that the Wild Man has settled down."

The elevator doors opened, but Denton didn't move. He folded his arms across his chest and frowned at Rachel. "If you ask me, Garret has done more to change you than vice versa. I don't call that being tamed."

The man would obviously do anything to keep from losing a bet, even twist the truth all around. "What are you talking about?" she asked. "Garret hasn't changed me."

Denton shook his head. "I've seen you at every Devils home game since you and Garret started dating. You're actually enjoying the games, even though I know you've always detested sports. And I hear you've kept that unruly beast of a dog of his—voluntarily. *And* you learned to play poker."

She hugged her arms across her chest and shifted her weight from one hip to the other. "I've expanded my interests into new areas," she said. "That doesn't mean I've changed in any significant way."

"I wouldn't call any of the so-called changes you listed for Garret significant, either."

"Then what about the fact that he hasn't been in the

penalty box in the past four games? That's definitely not the Wild Man he was before."

"You can't take credit for changing his style of play," Denton said.

"I can and I will." She kept her eyes locked to his. "You lost the bet, Denton. Now it's time to pay up. I want my own Man-Taming show."

"No." He moved past her, out of the elevator.

She hurried after him. "But why not? The column is already a hit. Just think of the ratings a television production could pull in."

He stopped so abruptly she almost collided with him. He turned to face her once more, a calculating gleam in his eyes. "I might give you the show on one condition."

"What's that?" Better not to appear too eager. Denton had never been known to make a deal that didn't work to his advantage. Which was all well and good as long as whatever he wanted didn't leave *her* at a disadvantage.

"You can have the show if you'll stop seeing Garret."

"What?" Her voice rose to a shriek. "You can't be serious."

"I am." He took a step toward her, his voice low and intense. "If you are responsible for the demise of Wild Man Kelly on the court—and that is a big if—then I don't want you influencing him any further. Break off the relationship and you get your show—and I'll get Wild Man back."

She stared at him, amazed at both his nerve and his cunning. "You're crazy," she said. "You can't intrude in my private life this way."

"You made it not-so-private when you agreed to the bet in the first place." He shrugged. "Take the deal or leave it."

"Leave it." But the words hurt to speak. Was she crazy to pass up her dream for the sake of a man whom she'd initially thought wasn't really her type? "What do you expect me to do—just dump him?"

"I'm sure you can come up with a way to let him down easy." He turned away again. "Call me when you've made up your mind," he said. "Then I'll talk to the station manager about your show."

She stared after him, unable to think of anything to say. Her stomach had tied itself in a knot and risen somewhere near her collarbone, where it stuck, a visceral reminder of how messy life could be when emotions and desires conflicted.

She wanted her own television show more than she'd ever wanted almost anything.

But she wanted Garret, too. The man was impossible, stubborn and aggravating, but in spite of all that he'd firmly captured her heart. How could she let him go without leaving a permanent hole inside her?

Maybe this was more proof than anything else Denton had cited that Garret *had* changed her. She'd fallen in love with the Wild Man—despite the fact that he wasn't her type.

Being in love ought to feel better than this, she thought as she made her way to her cubicle in the *Belinda* offices. Instead of elation, she felt only confusion. If she was in love with Garret, what did he feel for her? The other night he'd as good as admitted he loved her. How would he feel if he found out she'd begun dating him as part of a bet? Deceiving him when they were merely friends hadn't felt so awful, but now that her feelings went deeper, guilt twisted her insides.

Her man-taming principles weren't any help in a situation like this. Her focus had been on shaping men into the perfect spouses and boyfriends. She'd neglected to address what to do with them once they got that way— or how to deal with the changes they'd wrought in *you*.

She could admit now that Garret had changed her. He'd made her more willing to try new things, less uptight and more at ease with herself and those around her.

The phone on her desk rang and she snatched up the receiver. "Hello?"

"Hello, Rachel. It's Rhonda. I called to ask you to do me a favor."

Rachel blinked. Rhonda never called her at work. And Miss Cooly Confident never asked for favors from anyone. "What kind of favor?" she asked.

"I'm going to send you an invitation to the Winter Fantasy ball and I want you to come."

"Me? At your fancy society party?" Rachel laughed.

"It's a charity gala. And there will be lots of people there that you know. I'm sure Denton Morrison is on the guest list."

Right. As if she was in any mood to mingle with Denton just now. "Why do you want me to come?" she asked. "You've never asked me before."

"I just want you to be there, okay? And you can bring a date."

"Thanks." *I think.* She still wasn't sure she wanted to spend the evening watching a bunch of rich people in costume. Maybe Rhonda wanted her there so big sis could show off in her role as hostess.

"Are you going to bring that hockey player you've been seeing?" Rhonda asked.

"Lacrosse. Garret plays lacrosse. And if I bring anyone, it will be him. Why?"

"I want to meet him. You've been seeing him awhile now, I think it's time someone from the family met him."

"I'll be holding my breath, waiting for your approval."

"You don't have to be nasty about it."

Rachel winced. Rhonda was right. That had been nasty. And uncalled for. "I'm sorry. I—I'm just a little upset right now."

"Anything I can help with?"

"No, it's just…just something at work. It will work itself out. I'll come to the ball."

"It's a costume ball, so come up with something appropriate to a winter theme."

Rachel waited for Rhonda to lecture her to not be too outrageous or risqué, but for once big sis chose not to lecture.

"I'll find something," Rachel said. "And thanks for thinking of me. I appreciate it." It could be she didn't give Rhonda enough credit. Maybe she genuinely wanted Rachel to share her big night with her. And it might be fun to mingle with the upper crust for one evening. In any case, the champagne and food were bound to be top-notch.

She hung up the phone, still unsettled by the general tone of the phone call. Rhonda had sounded anxious, which wasn't really like her. She was usually so sure of herself and her place in the world. She'd been that way all her life, even before she married Harrison MacMillan and his millions.

Rachel shrugged and booted up her computer. She couldn't waste any more time brooding. She had an article to write.

But her mind was in no mood to cooperate today. As she stared at the blank computer screen, her thoughts shifted back to the invitation to the ball. She'd have to convince Garret to come with her—and in costume.

Mmm. She smiled as she pictured him dressed as a skier, in tight stretch pants and a Nordic sweater. In her experience, men didn't usually like to play dress-up, though they would given the proper incentive. In this case, maybe the prospect of seeing her dressed in an ice skater's wispy costume or maybe as a sexy snowflake would be enough.

If not, there was always bribery or begging. Many a man had given in under the pressure of tearful pleading or the promise of sexual favors.

"DINNER WAS NICE," Moira said as she settled next to Dave on the sofa of his apartment. They'd eaten at a new Thai place down the street and had had a really great time. Things were going better for them lately. They'd had fun at the lacrosse game with Rachel the other night. Maybe they were over the rough patch in their relationship.

"I'm really looking forward to the play next Saturday," she said, snuggling up to him. "I've heard such great things about it." She had two tickets for a production of *The King and I* at the Dallas Theater Center and couldn't wait for what would no doubt be a very romantic evening. Dinner at a fancy place before the show, then two hours mesmerized by an epic love story, then back to her place to work on their own love story.

"Saturday night?" He turned to look at her. "I can't go Saturday night. It's the first round of playoffs for the Devils. Me and Ed have tickets."

She really couldn't believe what she was hearing. "Dave, you promised," she said. "The deal was, I'd go to the last lacrosse game with you and you'd come to the theater with me."

"Yeah, but I didn't know it was the same night as the playoff game." He settled back against the sofa once more. "Get one of your girlfriends to go with you."

He tried to put his arm around her and she shoved away, angry tears clogging her throat. Okay. She was not going to cry in front of him. She had a lot to say and tears would only get in the way. "What is it with you?" she asked. "Lately I think you care more about some damn sports team than you do me."

"Sports and you are two different things." He wore a pained expression.

"You certainly spend more time watching sports than you do with me."

He sat forward, leaning toward her. "Maybe that's because I don't like being ragged on so much."

"What do you mean?"

"You should hear yourself." His voice rose to a falsetto. "'Dave, don't wear that shirt. Wear the green one instead.' 'Dave, your apartment is such a mess.' 'Dave, turn off the TV and take me dancing.'" He glared at her. "Don't think I don't know what you're doing."

"What am I doing?" Except trying to make their relationship better.

"You're trying out that man-taming crap your friend Rachel writes about. I tell you, it's not going to work on me."

She felt sick to her stomach. "I don't know what you're talking about." But her blush betrayed her.

"I'm not stupid, Moira. And I won't be trained like a dog. You either love me as I am or you don't love me at all."

"I *do* love you." She swallowed past the lump in her throat. "But I'm not so sure you love me. Not if you're not willing to do something as simple as change your shirt or clean your apartment to please me."

He shook his head. "I shouldn't have to worry about pleasing you. Love isn't about being happy with someone only if they do exactly what you want them to do."

She stood and backed away from the sofa, needing to put some physical distance between them. "You say that and yet you want me to let you watch sports all you want and never go out and sit around a sty of an apartment in ratty clothes and be a happy, compliant little woman. And I won't do it." She hugged her arms across her chest and inhaled a choking breath.

"Then I guess we don't have anything else to say to each other."

She stared at him, his words settling over her like

sleet, until she was chilled to the bone. Was this how love ended, with two people who couldn't even communicate on the same wavelength? Dave thought she wanted to make him into a different man altogether, when all she wanted was for him to acknowledge that she was important to him. That what she had to say mattered.

She had her answer now, didn't she? "I guess we don't," she whispered.

"Fine." He turned his back to her and picked up the television remote.

She stared at him, almost overwhelmed by the urge to lash out at him—to physically strike him. That he would dismiss her so lightly—actually turn his back on her—was the final blow. How could she love a man who had so little regard for her?

She picked up her purse and headed for the door, trying to think of some final, cutting remark. A fitting close to the scene.

But she could think of nothing. Her mind was filled with a gray fog. Only in movies were there perfect endings. In real life things were much messier and more painful.

"I FEEL LIKE A bleeding idiot." Garret scowled at the fake bearskin tunic and leather sandals he'd been given to wear for the photo shoot.

"Join the club." Bud, dressed in a fake tigerskin loincloth, hefted a foam club. "Too bad this isn't real. We could storm Denton's office and beat some sense into him with it."

"Aw, this isn't so bad." Guy Clifford joined them. "It's better than the ad we did where we were all in devil suits with pitchforks." He glanced down at his own costume. "I kind of dig the caveman look."

"What's that you're wearing?" Garret asked, indicating the orange fake-fur outfit. "It looks like an orangutan."

"It's a lion." Guy punched his shoulder. "You know—king of the jungle?"

"King of the looney bin, maybe." Garret picked up his lacrosse stick and took a seat on a fake boulder in the middle of the set. "Let's get this over with."

"All right, everybody." The director, a nervous young man named Simon, clapped his hands over his head. "Take your places."

The others found their marks, either standing or sitting around Garret. A tall woman with very short brown hair handed them their props—clubs, bones and a few lacrosse sticks.

Simon stood before the camera and addressed them. "All right now, this is very simple. The voice-over says, 'Wild Man Kelly and the Dallas Devils bring a whole new meaning to untamed sport in their playoff battle with the Denver Mammoth.'"

Groans and catcalls greeted this announcement. Simon waved them away. "All you have to do is sit there and scowl at the camera. And you—" he pointed to Garret "—say, 'Devils Lacrosse—it's wild.' Let me hear you say it."

"Devils Lacrosse it's wild," Garret said with no inflection or change of expression.

"No, no, no. It's 'Devils Lacrosse'—pause— 'It's *wild!*' Try again."

Garret parroted the director, somehow managing to keep a straight face. He supposed he should be glad Denton hadn't decided to make him pose with a bone in his hair, or dragging some cavewoman by her hair—probably only because the team owner hadn't thought of it yet.

"All right, then. Let's go." Simon clapped his hands again and the camera's red light blinked on.

The sound of jungle drums filled the studio, then a deep voice intoned "Wild Man Kelly and the Dallas Devils bring a whole new meaning to untamed sport in their playoff battle with the Denver Mammoth."

"Devils Lacrosse—it's wild."

"Cut, cut! Garret, please. Wait until I point to you."

"All right. I'll get it this time." He shifted on the rock. It was damned uncomfortable. Not to mention this bearskin was drafty.

"Devils Lacrosse—it's wild."

"More expression next time, Garret."

"Devils Lacrosse—it's wild!"

"Too much expression that time. Try again."

"Devils Lacrosse—it's *wild.*"

"Almost there, but not quite."

Garret growled in frustration."

"Ooh, I love that! Try adding that in."

"Devils Lacrosse—it's *wild*—grrrr."

"Oh, yes, that's perfect!"

Garret tossed aside the lacrosse stick and stood. "It bloody well better be because that's all you're getting out of me." He stalked off the set toward the dressing room. He needed some comfortable clothes and a cold beer. And he needed to have another talk with Denton.

Being known as the Wild Man had been fun at first. He liked being thought of as an intimidating, no-holds-barred player. But the shtick was getting old, and Denton was taking things too far. Garret chafed at being pushed into a mold this way.

Why was Denton—and the public—so hung up on image anyway? It was the same with all these women who glommed onto Rachel's Man Taming column. Instead of finding the man who was right for them and loving him for who he was, they believed they could take any man and turn him into Mr. Right by manipulating him a certain way.

Thank God, Rachel didn't try any of those tricks with him. Oh sure, she nagged him about his house-keeping and his clothes, but that was just part of being a woman. They had some extra gene or something—the same one that made girl babies talk earlier and caused grown women to be attracted to shoes.

If he could only convince Denton to see him as something other than the Wild Man. Couldn't he simply be Garret Kelly, all-star lacrosse player? Or Garret Kelly, Team Captain of the Dallas Devils?

Deep down inside, he knew Rachel liked him for himself. The two of them were good together, despite their differences. She'd been a good sport about trying new things, like taking care of his dog and learning to play poker. And he didn't really mind picking up his apartment for her. That's what love was all about, after all—making accommodations for each other.

For everything he gave up for Rachel, he gained so much more. Being with her made him a better person. He hoped she felt the same way about him. He was beginning to think she was the woman he wanted to spend the rest of his life with—a thought he'd never entertained before. The fact that the idea didn't make him break out in a cold sweat was a good sign, he thought. Any day now he'd work up the nerve to run the idea past her. One thing he knew about her—she'd be honest with him about her feelings. He loved that she didn't try to play games.

12

Man-Taming Principle Eight: Restrict Unwanted Behavior.

If compromise is truly the foundation upon which a good relationship is built, then this eighth man-taming principle is a shining example of compromise. If your significant other has a bad habit he refuses to relinquish, then attempt to come to an agreement that limits his indulgence in said habit, or restricts it to a particular time or place.

For instance, if he likes to smoke smelly cigars and you detest them, have him agree to only smoke outside or in cigar bars away from home. If his passion is poker, get him to agree to a once-a-month poker night with his pals. That horrible stuffed moose head you detest must stay in the garage, where he can visit it as much as he likes. You get the idea. You should also offer to restrict any of your own behaviors that disturb him— you'll only wash your pantyhose and hang them to dry in the laundry room. You'll only indulge in weepy chick-flick marathons when he's off playing poker with the guys. Everyone gets what he or she wants, but in limited doses. That's the beauty of compromise.

WHILE SHE DIDN'T really believe the way to a man's heart was through his stomach—she figured the true portal was a little farther south—Rachel reasoned a good meal would put Garret in the right mood for the three pieces of news she had to share with him: that she wanted him to accompany her to the Winter Fantasy ball, in costume; that Denton had asked her to stop seeing him; and oh yeah, that she'd been involved in this innocent little bet that was really just another one of Denton's publicity stunts and no harm done, right?

She only hoped rib eye steaks and turtle cheese-cake were enough to lull him into taking that last bit of news well.

When she answered his knock at six, he stepped inside and kissed her cheek. "Mmm. What smells so good?" he asked.

"It's my new perfume. It's called La Mirage."

"Does that mean it doesn't really exist?" He shook his head and moved past her, farther into the apartment. "No, this smells like steak."

"Rib eyes. I just put them on the grill." She led the way toward the balcony off the kitchen. "How do you like yours cooked?"

"Rare." He lifted the lid on the grill and checked the steaks, then reached for a fork. "A couple minutes on the other side and they'll be just right."

"I like mine a little more well done," she said.

He shrugged. "Suit yourself." He flipped both steaks

over, then moved his steak away from the fire and replaced the lid.

"There's Foster's in the fridge," she said. "And would you pour me a glass of Merlot?"

He came back with the drinks and they sat side by side on the glider on the balcony. "So how was your day?" she asked.

"After today, I really need this beer," he said. He took a long drink.

"Why? What happened?"

"We filmed a commercial. Denton had us dressing up like a bunch of cavemen."

"You mean like, animal skins and clubs?" She giggled.

"Exactly."

She laughed out loud. "I'll bet you were really cute." Come to think of it, the idea of him wearing nothing but a few scraps of fur and leather sent a pleasant warmth through her.

"Laugh if you want." He took another drink. "I've never felt so ridiculous."

"So how would you feel about dressing up like a skier?" she asked.

He looked puzzled. "It's April. I don't think there are many ski resorts open now. At least not in the northern hemisphere."

"It's for the Winter Fantasy ball. We've been invited."

"The big shindig your sister's heading up?"

"That one. It's a costume ball. We have to dress as something to do with winter."

He looked puzzled. "Shouldn't a Winter Fantasy ball be in the winter?"

"It was originally scheduled for February but they had to move it because of some mix-up with the ballroom."

"Then why didn't they change it to a Spring Fantasy ball?"

"I don't know. Maybe the decorations had already been ordered. So will you come with me?" She put her hand on his arm. "You don't have to dress in ski clothes if you don't want. You could be a Viking or something."

"I'll stick with the skiing. The Viking sounds too close to the caveman." He shook his head. "Of course, Denton would probably love that."

"Speaking of Denton, I spoke with him yesterday."

"Oh? What did he have to say?"

"He asked me to stop seeing you."

Garret choked on his beer. When he'd finished coughing, he stared at her. "He did what?" he gasped.

"He wants me to stop seeing you."

"I get it." He nodded. "He couldn't get me to break things off, so he went after you. The bastard."

She stared into her own drink. "He tried to bribe me, actually. Said I could have my own television show if I broke it off with you."

"I take it you told him no. Or is this dinner the lead up to a big kiss-off scene?"

"I told him no."

His smile held all the warmth of the Australian desert. He set aside his beer and reached for her. "Now that definitely deserves a kiss."

Before she could say more his lips covered hers. It was a kiss designed to make her forget about anyone or anything but this moment in time. His lips laid claim to hers, his tongue plundered her mouth, his whole body embraced her, leaving her dizzy and breathless. Was his ardor due to his relief that she hadn't accepted Denton's bribe? Did he love her that much? Her heart beat faster at the thought.

He'd progressed to sliding his hand beneath her shirt when she squirmed away from him. "The steaks," she said.

"Right." He stood and went to the grill. "Perfect," he said, checking the cooking meat. "If you'll hand me a platter, I'll serve them up."

She didn't want to spoil the mood during dinner, so she kept quiet about her third big revelation. When he was mellow on steak and cheesecake she'd tell him about the bet. With any luck they'd laugh it off.

"Was this commercial you made today to promote the playoff game?" she asked as they settled across from each other at her dining table.

"Yep." He cut into his steak. "We should have a huge turnout, making the playoffs our first year and all."

"Are you nervous about the game?"

He shook his head, chewing. When he swallowed, he said. "There's an adrenaline rush, sure. But if we play the way we've played all year, we can win."

"That's great."

He slathered butter on a slice of bread. "Tell me more about this television show Denton offered you. Is that something you're interested in?"

She nodded. "I'd love to take the man-taming concept to TV. I'd have guests on to discuss relationships, answer questions from audience members, things like that."

"More man taming. I can see where Denton would love that. The man is crazy for anything that catches the public's attention."

"Exactly." She leaned toward him, seeing a chance to ease into the subject of the bet. "It's like his whole idea to pair us in the beginning. The Man Tamer and the Wild Man."

"And now he can't stand that things worked out a little too well, can he?" His eyes met hers, silently telegraphing just how pleased he was with the way things had worked out between them.

Afraid she'd lose her resolve altogether if he kept staring at her that way, she looked away. "Yes, I don't think he anticipated us getting together."

"You know what they say. Opposites attract." He pushed back his chair and stood. "And I'd say we attract right well indeed."

"Uh-huh." She licked her lips, aware he was moving toward her. "About this whole Man Tamer and Wild Man scheme of Denton's. He thought it would be a good idea to make a little bet with me."

"I don't want to hear about Denton anymore." He took her hand and pulled her into his arms. "I've been looking forward to being alone with you all day."

The heat in his kiss made clear just how much he'd been looking forward to their time alone. "We…we should clean up," she protested weakly when she was able to break free. In fact they had a lot to clean up between them before she'd be truly comfortable.

"I'll help you with the dishes later. Right now all I want to do is take you to bed."

The urgency in his voice made her weak in the knees. Even guilt was no match for that kind of persuasion. She wrapped her arms around him, surrendering. "All right. Cleanup can wait."

"I love it when you're a dirty girl," he murmured in her ear.

"That's me. A dirty girl." Maybe just a little dingy around the edges.

"Speaking of costumes, I've been thinking about that dominatrix getup you wore a few weeks ago," he said. He grinned, a look that could melt stone. "Just remembering it makes me hot."

He guided her hand to his erection so she could feel just how hot he was. "I wasn't much of a dominatrix," she said.

"I think that's why it was such a turn-on. You looked totally hard-core, but you're really not much of a man tamer at all."

Maybe not a man tamer with a whip, she thought, but she'd done pretty well with him. "Don't tell anyone," she said. "You'll ruin my reputation."

Her voice turned breathy as Garret stuck his tongue in her ear. He loved how responsive she was to his touch. The longer he knew her, the more he found to love about her.

"I think playing the caveman for the afternoon today really turned you on," she said.

"You think so?" He hadn't felt particularly sexy in that fake bearskin—just ridiculous.

"Yeah. I think it put you in touch with your really wild side."

More likely it was *her* who brought out his animal nature. "I'll show you wild, woman."

She yelped as he scooped her into his arms and turned toward her bedroom. "What are you doing?" she said.

"I'm going to ravish you like the wild man I am."

She squirmed in his arms, arousing him further as she rubbed against him. He bent his head and took her nipple in his mouth, sucking hard, giving in to the urge to play a little rough. The idea of letting go, of trading restraint for raw lust, held a powerful pull tonight.

She moaned and he felt his response right in his groin. He grasped her more securely and strode into the bedroom. "What would you say if I said I wanted to rip the clothes from your body and make love to you until neither of us could walk?" He deposited her on the bed and leaned over her, looking deep into her eyes.

"I…." She wet her lips, eyes dilated. "Oh my."

He slipped his hand beneath her skirt and tugged at her panties, intending to pull them down. Instead, he felt the fabric give and tear. Her eyes widened and he had trouble breathing evenly. "I'll buy you another pair," he said as he tossed the ruined fabric aside. "Ten more pairs." He buried his face in her neck and cupped her mons, the sensation of softness, moisture and heat making his balls tighten and his cock throb.

She wore a halter blouse and no bra, and a short, tight skirt that emphasized the curve of her ass. The outfit had distracted him all evening, as no doubt it was designed to do. He cupped her breast through the thin fabric and felt the nipple pebble in his palm.

"Don't rip this," she said, reaching for the button at the neck.

"Not yet." He put his hand over hers, stopping her. Then he lowered his head and traced the outline of the nipple with his tongue. With each movement the fabric scraped against the sensitive tip and she let out a small cry.

Still laving her breasts, he undid the button of her skirt and helped her slide out of it. She was naked below the waist now, the triangle of dark gold hair framed by her pale thighs presenting an enticing picture.

She squirmed out of his grasp and sat up, reaching for the waistband of his jeans.

"All right, then," he said. He straightened and held out his hands.

Her smile was positively greedy as she sat up and undid the top button of his jeans. She slid four fingers beneath the waistband, brushing the hair above his penis, her touch light and teasing.

"Get on with it," he said, his voice a low growl.

She laughed, a sound as soft as a sigh. "Impatient, aren't you?"

"The word *ravish* does not imply patience."

"Hmm. I see your point." She lowered the zipper. As the fabric parted his erection tented the front of his shorts. She slid one long nail down the length of him, the not-so-gentle touch sending a new surge of desire through him.

He grasped his jeans and shorts and shoved them to the floor, then kicked out of them, along with his socks and shoes. "Enough with taking things slowly."

She laughed and took off her top, her breasts swaying slightly as she freed them, the motion mesmerizing. Her nipples were a deep pink and very erect, the skin slightly puckered around them. "And what is it you're in such a hurry to get?" she asked. She lay back against the pillows, legs coyly together, her attitude teasing.

Hands on her thighs, he parted her legs and knelt between them, the scent of her arousal rising to him. She was very wet, as anxious as he was, it seemed. "I'm in a hurry to get you," he said, urging her legs farther apart. "To get you writhing and moaning beneath me, screaming my name as you come."

"I never scream," she said.

He grinned. "Then who was that carrying on like a crazed cockatoo last time we made love? Not that I'm complaining, mind you."

"I screamed?" She looked mortified.

"Yes. And I'd like to hear it again." He punctuated the sentence with a thrust deep inside her. Her eyes lost focus and her expression went slack as he began to move with firm, sure strokes.

When he licked his thumb and brought it to rest against the hard bud of her clit she moaned and arched against him. He wished he had extra arms, so that he could both stimulate her and hold her close, exciting her as much as she excited him.

He slid one hand under her bottom to lift her, and increased the pressure on her clit. Her eyelids drooped and her breathing came in ragged gasps. Every small, mewling sound sent a jolt of desire straight to his groin. He could feel her tightening around him, and his concentration slipping away, but he forced himself to focus on her. "Come on, baby," he whispered. "Let go. Let me hear you scream."

He drove deeper into her, rapidly stroking her clit. Her cries grew louder. Her climax rocked him with an explosion of sound and sensation. "Gar-ret!" she cried, arching higher still.

Her whole body quivered in his hand, and he no longer tried to hold back his own release. He rode the sensation like a wave, until he was slammed into the beach, exhausted and struggling to breathe, but buoyed by elation.

He lay atop her, supporting his weight on his bent forearms, trailing kisses across her forehead, eyes still closed, savoring the aftershocks of pleasure that continued to buzz through him.

Only when their breathing had returned to normal did he open his eyes to find her looking up at him. "I screamed," she said.

"Yes, you did." He kissed her cheek, a tender brush of his lips. "It was beautiful."

"You're amazing, did you know that?"

He smiled. "I love you, Rachel Westover. What do you think of that?"

Her mouth formed a perfect O and she blinked rapidly, her eyes suspiciously shiny. "I love you, too," she whispered. "I really do."

"I know you do." Right here, right now, he was as sure of their feelings for each other as he'd ever been sure of anything in his life. It could be that the Wild Man had finally met his match.

LIKE A TRUE FRIEND, Rachel responded to the news of Moira and David's breakup with equal parts sympathy and indignation. "How horrible for you," she said when Moira told her the whole story over iced lattes after work on Monday. "I can't believe he would do that. You were the best thing that ever happened to him. He is so going to regret this."

"I can't believe it, either." Moira sighed and pinched a corner off a chocolate croissant. "I thought I knew him, and then to have him act this way."

"And over a ball game."

"It wasn't just the ball game," Moira said. "He said all this stuff about how I needed to accept him just as he was and not try to change him." She glanced at Rachel. "He was angry because I'd been using your man-taming principles on him."

"No, he was angry because he couldn't have you and do everything just the way he'd always done it. He wanted you to cater to him, to be the one to make all the sacrifices." Rachel took a long pull on her straw. "Relationships don't work that way," she added. "To think otherwise is selfish and immature."

"You're right," Moira said. "I think I've known that about him for a long time, I just didn't want to admit it."

Rachel nodded. "When you're in love you always want to see the person you love in the best light."

"Yeah. And then something like this happens and you see their true colors." As long as she lived, Moira would never forget the way David had turned his back on her, as if her leaving meant nothing. She straightened her shoulders and told herself she ought to be thankful she'd seen this side of him before she was tied to him by marriage or children.

Rachel leaned over and squeezed Moira's hand. "You'll find the man for you," she said. "You're a wonderful person and some smart guy is going to recognize it."

"Yeah, but when? I'm getting really tired of waiting. Not to mention the whole biological clock thing."

"If I knew that I'd quit writing my column and go into business as a fortune teller," Rachel said.

"Let's not talk about it anymore." Moira finished the last of the croissant. She'd eaten the whole thing without even realizing it. Since her break with David she'd been mainlining chocolate. She needed to get a grip. "How are things with you and Garret?"

"Good." Rachel hesitated. "Really good."

The look of pure bliss Rachel couldn't quite hide was enough to make Moira sick with jealousy. But she was a better friend than that. "What happened?" she asked. "You can tell me. I want you to be happy. Besides, if I can't have a decent relationship of my own, I can live vicariously through you."

Rachel's smile blossomed. "Saturday night, he told me that he loved me."

"Oh, Rachel." Happiness for her friend edged out jealousy. "That's wonderful."

Rachel nodded. "I can hardly believe it. It's been so long since I even allowed myself to think about the possibility of love, and now…" She shook her head. "Somebody pinch me."

"So he wasn't upset about the whole bet with Denton?" Rachel had shared her plans to confess all to Garret.

The smile faded a little. "Well…I didn't exactly tell him."

"Rachel!"

"I tried. I really did. But he kept turning it into a joke, and then he started kissing me and…" She blushed. "One thing led to another and I never got around to it." She stirred her drink with her straw. "It doesn't matter anyway, since Denton isn't going to pay up on the bet."

"What if Garret finds out about the bet from someone else?"

"He won't. Besides, he's a typical man, convinced man taming would never work on him—even though it has."

"Maybe it wasn't man taming," Moira said. "Maybe it was love all along. And that's why the principles didn't work on Dave. Because what we had wasn't really love." Her voice caught on these last words and she hurried to gulp down her latte.

"I'll admit a man in love probably has more incentive to want to please the woman," Rachel said. "But behavior modification has been proven to work in all kinds of situations and relationships."

"Well, I'm really happy things are working out so well for you. It gives me hope. If you can be happy with someone so different from you, maybe the right man for me is someone I never even considered before." It was a comforting thought.

Rachel laughed. "Yeah, who would have ever thought I'd end up dating a jock?" A dreamy look came into her eyes. "But he really is a great guy."

"Yeah." *And somewhere there has to be a great guy for me,* Moira thought. *I just need to hang on to that hope.* "Want to go to the theater Saturday night?" she asked. "I've got two tickets to *The King and I.*"

"I can't." Rachel shook her head. "I'm sorry, but it's the championship game and I promised Garret I'd be there. And he's going to Rhonda's stuffy party with me, so I have to be at the game."

"I understand. I probably should just try to sell the tickets. This was supposed to be a big romantic evening for me and Dave. Going without him would just remind me of what might have been."

"Why don't you come to the game with me?" Rachel said. "Garret can get us great seats. It'll be fun."

"I don't think so," Moira said. "Dave will be there."

"So? You should go just to show him you don't care."

"He'll think I'm following him."

"No, he'll see you there having a good time and he'll realize what an idiot he was to ever let you get away. I wouldn't be surprised if he didn't beg you to take him back."

The thought made Moira queasy. "I'm not sure I want him back." But would she be strong enough to resist him if he came after her?

"All the better," Rachel said. "You'd have the satisfaction of telling him to get lost." She leaned toward Moira. "Come with me. It'll be fun."

"I don't know…"

"It's a big arena. You probably won't even see Dave. And what else are you going to do? Sit at home and brood?"

"Probably." And eat. She sucked in her stomach. Keep this up and she'd have to buy new clothes. "Okay, I'll go," she said. "But I can't be responsible for what I might say if I do see Dave." Odds were she'd either burst into tears or tell him exactly what she thought of his sorry behavior—or both.

"Don't worry, I've got your back," Rachel said. "And if he gives us any trouble, I know a few lacrosse players who'd be happy to teach him a few manners."

The thought of Dave being attacked by a bunch of large men with lacrosse sticks almost made her smile. Maybe she was on her way to getting over him after all.

13

Man-Taming Principle Nine: Reward Good Behavior.

The very basis of Man Taming is positive reinforcement. Though the principle of rewarding good behavior is number nine on the list, it may be the technique you use most frequently, and with the most success. It's also very simple: when your man does something you like, reward him. The reward can be in the form of praise, a back rub, a compliment, or something as simple as a smile.

It's human nature to crave positive feelings and experiences. We will do anything to seek them out. The subconscious learns very quickly what actions provoke positive responses and will repeat these actions in hopes of being rewarded. Your job then, dear reader, is to make sure you are ready with the rewards.

COMING HERE TONIGHT had been a mistake. Moira knew that the minute she walked into the sports stadium and saw Dave waiting in line for beer. Fortunately, he didn't spot her. She ducked behind a pillar and stood there, shaking.

"Moira? What are you doing?" Rachel peered around the pillar at her.

"What does it look like I'm doing? I'm hiding." She ducked her head. If she couldn't see Dave, maybe he wouldn't notice her.

"Hiding from whom?" Rachel looked around.

"Dave. He's over there in the beer line."

"So?" Rachel tugged her arm. "Don't be silly. Walk by as if you never noticed him. You certainly don't have to speak with him."

"I shouldn't be here at all." Moira refused to move. "I want to go home."

"Come on." Rachel tugged harder, succeeding in pulling her from behind the pillar. "You're going to have a good time and you're going to forget all about what's-his-name."

Moira glanced over at the beer line. No sign of Dave. She reluctantly allowed Rachel to pull her along. Hordes of rowdy fans crowded around them, many wearing Dallas Devils T-shirts and jerseys, some with their faces painted in the Devils' colors of red and black. As the women settled into their seats right behind the players area, a group of fans to their left unfurled a banner that read Go Devils, Slaughter The Mammoth.

"I can't believe people can be this crazy about a sport," Moira said.

"I guess that's why they call them fanatics." The players were on the floor taking their warmup. Rachel waved to Garret, who saluted her with his lacrosse stick. The man next to him waved, also.

"Who's that?" Moira asked, assessing the other player. He had sandy hair, blue eyes and a nice smile. "He looks familiar."

"That's Bud Mayhew. You've met him before. At Denton's party."

"Right." She smiled. How could she have forgotten the man who defended her honor, so to speak, in the wake of Dave's neglect?

Someone else in the players' area caught her attention. "Speaking of Denton," she said. "Why is he giving you the evil eye?"

Rachel glanced at her boss, then looked away. "He's mad because he told me to stop seeing Garret and I refused."

"He told you to stop seeing Garret? Why?"

"He thinks it's bad for the Wild Man's image to be tied to one woman. Especially a woman who writes a column called The Man Tamer."

Moira shook her head. "Isn't he the one who set you two up to begin with?"

"Yes, but only because he thought we wouldn't take— since we had nothing in common. Or so he thought."

"You didn't think you had anything in common, either," Moira said.

"Not on the surface, maybe, but inside, where it counts, I think we're a lot alike." Her smile was dreamy. So happy it made Moira's heart ache.

She looked away, only to spot Dave across the arena. He was seated next to his friend Ed, but was currently talking in an animated fashion to a busty brunette in a Devils jersey. "So much for thinking he's pining away for me," she muttered.

"What was that?" Rachel asked.

"I don't think Dave is exactly heartbroken over me leaving him." She nodded in his direction.

Rachel frowned. "Maybe he saw you and is trying to make you jealous."

Moira shrugged. "Forget about him. I don't care anymore." Her heart still hurt when she thought about Dave, but it no longer felt permanently broken.

Loud rock music announced the players' entrance and the crowd erupted in a deafening roar as fireworks exploded. The Dallas Devils, Garret in the lead, ran onto the court and the crowd rose for the national anthem.

Moira focused on the game, determined not to look at Dave. She didn't care about him anymore. Time to get on with her life.

The Devils scored first. The crowd went crazy and never fell silent after that. Moira let herself get caught up in the excitement, cheering when one of the Devils players blocked a Mammoth shot or intercepted the ball, jumping to her feet when the Devils scored another goal.

Bud Mayhew scored four goals. Moira found herself watching for him on every play. He seemed to be always smiling. And he had great legs….

Two beers, three sponsor giveaways, a giant pretzel, a halftime performance by the Devil Dancers, eight penalties and two fights later, the Dallas Devils defeated the Denver Mammoth 17-11. The stadium shook with the noise from the crowd. Women screamed and strangers hugged each other.

Rachel pushed through the crowd, Moira in her wake. They ended up in the hallway outside the players' locker room, where Rachel greeted Garret with a hug.

Moira folded her arms and looked around, a nervous smile on her face. Bud Mayhew saw her and came over. "Hey," he said.

"Hey," she answered. "Congratulations on winning. You played a good game."

"Thanks." He looked around, then back at her. "It's Moira, isn't it? It's good to see you again."

"It's good to see you, too, Bud." Her smile this time was genuine. He really did have the nicest eyes. They looked…kind. She could use a little kindness right now.

"So…you here by yourself?" he asked.

"I'm here with Rachel." She nodded toward Rachel and Garret, who were still embracing.

"Oh. You're with Rachel. I thought…the last time I saw you, you were with a guy."

"Dave. We're not dating anymore. I'm not seeing anyone in particular right now." The words felt…liberating. She smiled. "What about you, Bud? Do you have a wife or girlfriend waiting to celebrate your victory with you?"

His face flushed. "Nah. Not me." He juggled his lacrosse stick from hand to hand. "So…do you come to games often?"

"No. I had fun tonight, but I'm really not that into sports."

"That's okay. There are a lot more important things in life."

This from an athlete? She moved a little closer. "What do you do when you're not playing lacrosse?" she asked.

"I'm a teacher. Fourth grade."

Her heart beat a little faster. "That must be a challenge."

"The kids are great. Though sometimes the parents…" He laughed. "No, really, I love my job."

"I'll bet every girl in class has a crush on you."

That blush again. Who knew modesty could be so sexy?

The crowd around them thinned and Bud looked over his shoulder. "I have to get to the locker room," he said. "Nice talking to you."

"You, too." She hesitated a moment as he turned away, then she called out to him. "Bud?"

He turned toward her once more. "What is it?"

She pulled a grocery receipt from her purse and scrawled her name and phone number on it. "Why don't you call me sometime?"

He grinned and accepted the paper. "Yeah. Yeah, I'll do that."

She smiled and turned away, humming to herself. Strange how an evening that started out so badly could end so well.

AS RACHEL AND GARRET joined the throng of people streaming into the Quorum Ballroom, she had to remind herself she hadn't stepped into some alternate reality.

All around her were men and women dressed in costumes that featured an abundance of expensive fur, silver lace and conspicuous diamonds. In her own Michelle Kwan ice skater's ensemble she felt downright plain. "I hate this kind of thing," she said.

"You do?" Garret sounded surprised. "I thought all women loved big fancy parties." He adjusted the ski goggles that rested atop his head. "Especially when they involve a chance to make the man in their life feel ridiculous."

The man in her life. The words sent a pleasant warmth through her. "You look great," she said. The blue-and-white, Nordic-patterned sweater emphasized his broad shoulders and trim waist, while the tight ski pants accented his perfect butt. "I'll probably have to beat back the other women with a ski pole."

She glanced toward the entrance to the building again. A Viking was escorting a woman who looked alarmingly like Cruella de Vil through the door, followed by a pair of Abominable Snowmen. "No, it's not the dressing up I hate, it's the pretension," she said. "This whole evening is about people with money trying to impress other people with money."

"You have something against people with money?" he asked.

"Not at all. Just pretentious people in general."

"Come on." He offered her his arm. "We'll show them we're not impressed."

They made their way up the steps into the ballroom. The cavernous space was hung with thousands of icicle lights and silver tinsel. White-trunked trees trimmed with more lights lined the room and giant snowflake ice sculptures formed the centerpieces for refreshment tables along the back wall. A small dais and speaker's podium had been set up at the front of the room. A string quartet dressed in white tuxes played classical music and white-tuxed waiters circulated with trays of champagne and hors d'oeuvres. Rachel searched for her sister, but in the crush it was impossible to find anyone. "I don't see Rhonda," she said.

"What is she wearing?" Garret asked.

"I don't know. She wouldn't tell me. Though I think I convinced her not to go through with her Frost Queen idea."

They moved farther into the room, bumping up against snowmen, a man in a Santa Claus suit and several men in black tuxes. "I need a drink," Garret said as he stared after Santa Claus.

"Good idea," Rachel said. She snagged a couple of glasses of champagne from a passing waiter.

She offered one to Garret, who made a face. "No, I mean a *real* drink." He nodded toward the opposite end of the room. "I think there's a bar over there. Do you want to come with me?"

"No, I'll stay here and look for Rhonda." It might be a good idea to talk with her sister before she met Garret—warn her not to go into interrogation mode or do something stupid like ask him his intentions. She wouldn't put it past Rhonda to play the family matriarch, though she was only six years older than Rachel.

She sipped champagne and studied the passing women. A surprising number weren't wearing real costumes at all—merely ball gowns in shades of silver and white, with masks and shimmery jewelry. The effect was somewhat icy, but lacked creativity.

Rhonda had probably resorted to something similar. Safe and dull. Heaven forbid her sister risk offending anyone.

A slight commotion behind her made her turn around. She smiled as she watched a woman make her way through the crush of people. In her wake men whistled or clapped and women murmured. Now here was someone not afraid to cause a stir, Rachel thought. The woman's costume consisted of a clinging silver gown, cut out to reveal a flat stomach accented with a diamond in her navel. More diamonds accented her bare shoulders and the deeply dipping neckline of her dress. A sparkly headdress/mask framed the woman's face. The overall effect was of a human icicle—ironic considering how hot the woman looked.

This is someone I have to meet, Rachel thought as she headed toward the woman. Together they could gossip about all the stuffy men and women around them.

As she drew closer, the icicle woman looked up and met Rachel's gaze. A flush of red washed her pale cheeks and Rachel stopped in her tracks as recognition hit her with the force of a punch in the gut. She closed her eyes, opened them again, and stared. The woman hurried toward her.

"Rhonda?" Rachel gasped when they were face to face.

Rhonda looked around nervously. "Shh. My identity is supposed to be a surprise."

"It's a surprise all right." Rachel grinned. "You look amazing."

Rhonda smoothed the form-fitting gown over her hips. "Do you think it's all right?"

"It's fantastic." She took a step back to get a better look. "My God, you look ten years younger. I'd kill for a figure that great."

Rhonda's smile was less uncertain. "Thanks. I guess all that time in the gym was good for something."

"Has Harrison seen you? What does he think?"

Rhonda shook her head. "He hasn't seen me yet. I told him I'd meet him here." She stood on tiptoe and searched the room.

"What is he wearing?" Rachel asked. "I'll help you look."

"A tuxedo."

"I thought this was a costume ball."

"I reminded him of that," Rhonda said. "He said he was in costume. He's dressed as a penguin."

Rachel laughed. "That sounds like Harrison." Her brother-in-law had a dry wit that belied his overly dignified outward appearance.

"Where's your date?" Rhonda stopped searching the ballroom and looked at Rachel. "I thought you were bringing your lacrosse player—the Wild Man."

"Garret went to get a drink at the bar." She looked in the direction he'd disappeared, but of course couldn't see him from here. "I hope we can find each other again in this madhouse." She turned to Rhonda. "Promise me when you meet you won't ask him a lot of questions."

"What kind of questions?"

"You know—personal questions. About his family or his intentions or anything like that."

Rhonda frowned. "Is there something about his family you don't want me to know?"

"No! I just don't want him to feel like he's being grilled or anything. Just…take some time to get to know him. He's a really great guy."

Rhonda studied her. "You really like him, don't you?"

She nodded. "I love him. And he loves me." She moved closer, her voice low. "I think this could really be something serious and I don't want to blow it."

Rhonda patted her arm with surprising tenderness. "Don't worry about me. I'm sure if you love him, I'll love him, too."

"Would Mr. and Mrs. Harrison MacMillan please come to the podium?" An announcement cut through the din.

"I have to go," Rhonda said. "I'm supposed to present a check to a representative from Children's Hospital." She hugged her arms under her breasts. "Oh my God, I forgot they'd be taking a picture for the paper. I hope this costume wasn't a mistake."

"You look wonderful." Rachel gave her a quick hug. "Go up there and knock them dead."

Rachel positioned herself so that she had a good view of the podium. Harrison reached the dais first and waited for his wife. Clearly, he didn't recognize the bombshell approaching, though Rachel noticed he did the thing all men did, where they look while pretending not to look.

Rachel saw the exact moment recognition hit him.

His mouth dropped open and his face went white, and he had to steady himself on a chair. Then a huge grin spread across his face, and he rushed to help Rhonda up the stairs to the speaker's area. "Does she know how to make an entrance or what?" he said, his words audible over the microphone on the podium.

The others on the podium laughed, some a little less enthusiastically than others. Then Rhonda was front and center, posing with an oversize check with a man and woman who represented the hospital. "On behalf of the Children's Hospital Auxiliary I'd like to present this check for $56,000," she said. Flashes strobed like a host of fireflies, everyone shook hands, then Rhonda stepped back to the microphone. "I'd like to welcome everyone to the seventeenth annual Winter Fantasy ball. I hope you all have a wonderful time. Now let's have a little fun, shall we?"

Curtains behind her parted to reveal a five-piece band, which immediately began playing "Baby, It's Cold Outside." Harrison grabbed his wife's hand and led her down from the dais onto the dance floor in front of the band and gathered her into his arms. The way he looked at Rhonda made Rachel sigh. How romantic.

Speaking of romance, where was Garret? Probably waylaid by some fan. She supposed she'd better get used to it. She set her empty champagne flute on a side table and headed toward the bar. Time to find her date and create a little fun of her own.

"COULDN'T YOU COME UP with a better costume than that?"

Garret was waiting for his drink at the bar when a

familiar voice accosted him. He turned to stare into the face mask of a hockey player, whom he realized with a start was Denton Morrison. "Who are you supposed to be?" Garret asked. "Wayne Gretzky?"

Denton removed his helmet. "Nobody's going to mistake you for Bode Miller, that's for sure," he said. He nodded to the bartender. "Dewar's, straight up," he ordered.

Garret accepted his drink and deposited a dollar in the tip jar. "Nice costume, Denton. Where'd you get it?"

"Where do you think? The owner of the Stars is a friend of mine." Denton collected his drink and moved away from the bar. Garret followed. "What are you doing at this horror show?" Denton asked, looking around.

Garret hesitated, then decided he had nothing to hide. "I'm here with Rachel. Her sister is in charge of this thing."

"Rhonda MacMillan?" Denton shook his head. "Hard to believe those two are sisters."

"I take it they're not much alike."

"Too bad. Rhonda MacMillan is one classy lady."

Garret bristled. "Are you suggesting Rachel doesn't have class?"

Denton waved his hand as if brushing aside Garret's irritation. "You know I think the world of Rachel. But she's not exactly dignified."

This from a man standing in the middle of a crowded ballroom wearing a hockey uniform. "What do you care if she's dignified or not?" Garret said. "Since when does dignified sell magazines?"

"You're right. I'm just thinking of her personally. Frankly, I'm not surprised she's still single. This whole man-taming thing has probably scared off any man who'd be interested in her."

"It hasn't scared me," Garret said.

Denton glanced at him. "If you had any sense it would."

Was this another ploy to split them up? Fat chance of it working. "I don't care what Rachel writes in her column," he said. "All that matters is how the two of us relate to each other. And we get along great." Better than he'd ever gotten along with any woman. Rachel was his friend as well as his lover—a combination he could see lasting a long time. Maybe even forever.

He took another drink to wash that thought down. *Slow down, mate,* he told himself. *No need to rush into anything.*

"Shows what you know." Denton's laugh was loud and raucous. Several people turned to stare, but he didn't notice. He nodded to Garret. "By God, she really has got your number, hasn't she?"

Garret frowned. "What do you mean?"

"She's been working her man-taming magic on you all this time and you never even realized it." He shook his head. "And you were the last person I thought she could do that to."

"What are you talking about?" Garret asked, a tightness growing in his chest. "What man-taming magic? That's just a column she writes."

"It may be just a column to you, but Rachel—and all her fans—believe in that stuff." Denton swallowed the last of his drink and handed the empty glass to a passing waiter. "She believes in it so much she bet me she could tame the Wild Man—you. And much as it pains me to admit it, it looks as if she's done just that." He sighed. "I'm really disappointed in you, Garret. I thought you were a better man than that or I'd never have agreed to such a ridiculous wager."

"Wager?" Garret felt sick to his stomach. He clenched his hands into fists. "Rachel made a *bet* with you?"

Denton nodded. "If she won, I agreed to give her her own Man Taming television show." He stared out across the ballroom. "I guess I'll have to pay up now."

"I can't believe she'd do such a thing."

Denton shrugged. "You know women when they want something. Rachel's been after me about this TV show for months. Maybe it won't be so bad. The column pulls in a lot of readers, though I'm still not sure how it will translate to television. I just hope I don't lose money on it."

Garret didn't give a damn about television, or about Denton's money worries. "Are you saying Rachel only went out with me to win a bet?" he asked.

"All I know is you're the first jock I've ever known her to date," Denton said. "She always went for the more sophisticated type before. You know, business suits, BMWs, that sort of thing." He put his hand on Garret's shoulder. "Sorry to break this to you. I would have thought she'd have had the decency to tell you by now."

No, she hadn't had the decency to tell him the truth. She'd led him around by his balls and he'd followed like a puppy. He'd believed it when she'd told him she loved him. He shook his head, trying to clear it, but he couldn't shake the gray fog that engulfed him. He let himself get trapped by an illusion—by the idea of a woman who loved him for himself, bad habits and all. When all along she'd only seen him as a sick social experiment. A prize to feed her ambition.

"Don't look so down," Denton said, his voice cheerful. "Away from her influence, you'll be your old self in no time at all. The Wild Man will return and we'll all be better off for it."

He glared at the older man. Just like Denton to turn this to *his* advantage. He turned away. "I need a drink." He'd need a whole lot of drinks to drown the pain he was feeling now. Worse, what would he say to Rachel when he saw her again?

RACHEL SPOTTED GARRET at the bar and hurried up to him. "There you are," she said. "Have you been waiting all this time for a drink? Did you see Rhonda? I couldn't believe how fabulous she looks." She laughed. "Maybe I've been a good influence on her."

Garret turned to her, his expression dark and forbidding. "That's what you'd like to think, isn't it?" he said, his voice a low growl. "That you can manipulate other people into doing what you want."

The venom in his voice confused her. She took a step back and stared at him. "What are you talking about? Garret, what's wrong?"

He looked at her the way he might look at a bug he wanted to squash beneath his heel. "I ran into Denton and he told me about your little bet." He tossed back a shot of liquor and shoved his empty glass across the bar, signaling for another.

She felt sick and cold. "It's not what you think," she said weakly.

"When were you going to tell me the truth? Or did you think you could continue to pull the wool over my eyes right up until the day you decided to dump me?"

"Dump you?" She shook her head. "Garret, I love you. Why would I dump you?"

"You loved the idea of your own television show. That's the only thing you loved." He shoved back from the bar. "I'm surprised it took me so long to see it."

He tried to move past her, but she grabbed his arm. "No!" she protested. "It's not like that at all."

His eyes met hers once more, no warmth in them. "So Denton made up everything about the bet?"

She swallowed. "No. There was a bet. But then I realized I loved you and—"

"You told him I wasn't your type."

"Yes, but that was before I knew you." Would every flip remark she'd ever made be used against her this way?

"So you fell in love with me and had no intention of collecting on your bet?"

"Yes. I mean no." She gripped him more tightly, fingers digging into the hard muscle. "Of course I still wanted the show. That was beside the point."

"To me, that is exactly the point. You used me and I don't appreciate it."

"Garret, please." She searched frantically for something to say to cool his anger. "I'll admit the bet was wrong. And I wanted to tell you the truth. I tried the other night, but the time was never right."

"Get away from me." He pried her hand from his

arm. "Your sister or someone can take you home. I never want to see you again."

He moved quickly away from her. She stared after him, tears blurring her vision, sobs stuck in her throat. She was dimly aware of people around her, staring, and she fought not to break down in front of them. But how could a person hurt so much and survive? Garret, who'd loved her—more than any man had ever loved her—now hated her.

And she had only herself to blame.

14

Man-Taming Principle Ten: Acceptance (The Last Resort)

In severe cases, you may find that a man does not respond to any of the man-taming principles. He refuses to give up his bad behavior in the face of both reward and punishment. In fact, he may become even more entrenched. Now the ball is once more in your court. You must decide—is the man in question worth putting up with his bad behavior?

Only you can make this decision. You may decide the bad behavior is outweighed by the man's good qualities. In this case, you may decide to accept the behavior and learn to live with it. If this principle is one you choose to employ, I urge you to adopt it wholeheartedly. There will be a temptation to slip and try once more to change it, but you've already proven that doesn't work. So adopt an attitude of true acceptance and move on.

RACHEL SLUMPED ON HER SOFA in front of the television and ate Lucky Charms out of a mixing bowl, shoveling the cereal into her mouth with a large soup spoon. The words of the two men in suits on the screen scarcely registered through the wall of her grief. A week had passed since that awful night at the Winter Fantasy ball and if anything she felt the loss of Garret more acutely than ever. She was beginning to doubt she'd ever recover. She might spend the rest of her life—or at least until her money ran out—seated right here on her sofa, paralyzed by sorrow.

The doorbell rang and she stared numbly at the door. The only people she'd seen all week were a pizza delivery boy and a nice young man witnessing for his church. The pizza deliverer had given her a sympathetic smile as he'd pocketed his tip, while the young man had stared at her in horror and quickly fled, not even bothering to leave one of his tracts behind.

The doorbell rang again, insistent. She sighed and hoisted herself off the sofa and shuffled over to look out the peephole. Moira stared back at her. "I know you're in there," Moira said. "Open up."

Rachel rested her forehead against the door. The wood felt cool and smooth, soothing even. She'd told Moira and her office she had the flu, then refused to answer the phone after that.

Even the flu would have felt better than this pain in her head and her heart that she couldn't shake.

The door rattled. "Let me in, Rachel, or I'm going to get the apartment manager to open it with his key."

Rachel sighed and unfastened the chain and opened the door. Moira rushed inside, then took a step back. "You look awful," she said.

Rachel glanced down at her chocolate-smeared pajamas. "I haven't felt like dressing up."

"Or taking a shower, either." Moira wrinkled her nose. "I heard what happened with you and Garret."

"How did you hear?" Was everybody talking about them now? Did they think the Man Tamer had gotten what she deserved from the Wild Man?

"A guy in my office works part-time for the caterer and he saw the whole thing. I'm sorry, hon."

Rachel's face crumpled. "I feel…so…so…awful!" she sobbed.

Moira gathered her into her arms and patted her back. "It's okay, hon. You'll be all right."

"No I won't," Rachel said. "I'll never be all right again. I l-l-*loved* him!" The thought brought forth a fresh surge of tears.

Moira led Rachel to the sofa and cleared a space for them both to sit, pushing aside a box of tissues, empty cereal bowls and a sad-looking stuffed bear. "What's this?" she asked, picking up the bear.

"That's Mr. Pickles." Rachel grabbed the bear and cuddled him close. "I've had him since I was four."

"Okay." Moira patted Rachel's arm and settled in next to her. "Tell me what's going on. I'm here to listen."

"Nothing's going on." She picked up the remote and aimed it at the television, turning down the sound. "Garret hates me. And I don't really blame him."

"I take it he found out about your bet with Denton."

Rachel nodded and focused on the television. The national anthem was playing. She sniffed back fresh tears.

"Denton told him. Now Garret thinks the only reason I ever dated him was to get my own television show."

"That is the main reason you dated him to begin with," Moira said.

"You're not helping," Rachel wailed.

"I'm sorry. I know you weren't even thinking about the bet when you fell in love with him. Were you?"

"Of course not!" She dabbed at her nose with a tissue and watched as players rushed onto the court to the beat of rock music.

"What are you watching?" Moira turned toward the television. "Is that lacrosse? Oh honey, don't torture yourself this way." She reached for the remote, but Rachel pulled it away.

"No. It's the semifinals. The Devils are playing the Arizona Sting. Even if Garret won't have anything to do with me, I can still cheer for him to win." She sniffed.

"You don't sound very cheerful to me," Moira said.

Rachel glared at her.

"All right, I'm sorry." Moira sat back and hugged a pillow to her chest. "I know this is tough for you. I came over to sympathize."

"Thanks." She stared at the television screen, attention zeroed in on Garret. He looked so good her heart hurt. When the camera zoomed in for a close-up she had to bite her lip to keep from crying out.

"Bud told me he's hoping for a six-point game tonight," Moira said.

"Bud?" Rachel turned to her friend. "When did you talk to him?"

Moira flushed. "We went out for coffee yesterday."

"You and Bud Mayhew?" Rachel sat up straighter, grateful for the distraction. "How did this come about?"

"While you were busy with Garret after the last game, I ran into Bud and we started talking." She smiled. "He's a really nice guy."

"What about Dave?" Rachel asked.

Moira looked away. "I'm still upset over the way things ended between us, but maybe I was lucky to break it off with him when I did. He didn't really appreciate me."

"You're right. He didn't," Rachel said. "When he didn't respond to any of my man-taming techniques I should have known he was a lost cause."

"Your man-taming techniques were part of the problem," Moira said.

Rachel blinked. "What do you mean? *Dave* was the problem, not my techniques."

"But if you hadn't convinced me man taming would work I wouldn't have wasted so much time with him." Moira's look was accusing. "I know you mean well, but maybe those techniques of yours do more harm than good. Maybe instead of telling women how to remake a man into the perfect partner, you ought to be telling them how to find a man who's *already* the perfect guy for them."

Rachel swallowed a fresh knot of tears. "But nobody is perfect," she said. "Everyone can be made better."

"But who says it's a woman's job to remake a man? Don't we all want to be loved for who we are already?" Moira tossed aside the pillow and leaned toward Rachel. "Maybe training a man like a dog isn't the most loving thing to do. Maybe the loving thing is to accept him, flaws and all. And hope that he'll accept us that way, too."

Rachel felt as if she'd swallowed rocks. "I—I always thought getting rid of bad habits would make it easier to love," she said. But then she'd fallen in love herself. And once love took over, hadn't Garret's sloppy clothes, messy apartment and big dog shrunk in importance as her admiration and respect for him as a person grew? There were weeks she hardly noticed the little things that had once bothered her. She'd thought this was evidence that her man taming had been a success.

But maybe the truth was that love made her look at Garret through different eyes. *He* hadn't changed as much as love had changed *her.* She buried her face in her hands and rocked forward. "I've been such an idiot."

Moira patted her back. "I think we're all idiots when it comes to love," she said.

"What am I going to do?" Rachel wailed. "I want him back, but he won't even speak to me."

"I don't know that there's anything you can do about that," Moira said. "You hurt his pride and that's probably the worst blow in the world for a man."

Rachel raised her head and sniffed. "I know. I feel so stupid."

"You're not stupid. You just made a mistake. Now all you can do is try not to make the same mistake again."

She nodded and scrubbed at her eyes with a wadded-up tissue. "I'm going to forget about man taming. And I'm going to tell Denton he can forget about the television show. He can run *Space Cadet Coeds* instead."

"But you're the Man Tamer. What will you do for a living if you don't have your column?"

"I'll write something else." She sat up straighter.

"After all, I still have my degree in psychology." And some hard-learned lessons about the dynamics between men and women. Maybe there was a way to use what she'd been through to help others avoid making the same mistakes she'd made.

She glanced at the television. The Devils were behind four to two. Garret was sitting in the penalty box, a scowl on his face. Denton had gotten what he wanted, then. The Wild Man was back.

But the Man Tamer was gone for good.

GARRET AND HIS TEAMMATES gathered at a downtown bar, mourning their loss with drink. Garret stared into his beer and berated himself. "If I'd kept my wits and hadn't gotten so many penalties, we would have had a chance," he said. He'd let this whole thing with Rachel get to him, to the point where it had affected his game. That had never happened to him before.

He didn't want to think about her, but he couldn't help it. He dreamed about her at night, and he was constantly seeing things that reminded him of her—an article in the paper she would have liked or a pair of her underwear in his apartment.

Whoever said love was bliss didn't understand it was closer to an illness or torture.

That was the worst of it, that he loved her still in spite of everything. Given enough time, he'd get over her, but right now he was living in hell.

"Wake up, Garret. I'm talking to you."

An elbow in his ribs jerked him from his moping. He glared at Bud. "What is it?"

"I said if splitting with Rachel has put you in such a bad mood, maybe you ought to see her again."

He shook his head. "She lied to me, mate. I could never trust her again."

"Technically, she didn't tell you the whole truth. Besides, don't tell me you never lied to a woman."

This wasn't another woman they were talking about. This was Rachel. "I never lied to Rachel," he said.

Bud shrugged. "I'm just saying maybe you ought to at least hear her side of things."

"Don't listen to him!" A voice from somewhere behind them cut in. They turned and saw Dave Brewer. He rose from his bar stool and came toward them, a little unsteady on his feet. He braced himself on the back of Garret's chair and leaned in close, smelling of beer and peanuts. "Don't go crawling back to her, man," he said. "Then she'll have you right where she wants you. We've got to stand up to these ball-busting women."

Bud scowled at Dave. "Who asked you?"

"Just offering the voice of experience," Dave said. "I know these man-taming women. They're never satisfied. They're always trying to change us. Makes me think they never wanted a real man in the first place."

Bud crushed a beer can in one hand. "What makes you such an expert?" he asked.

"I told you, man. I dated one of those women. She tried to change me." He tried to stand up straighter, swaying dangerously. "But I showed her. The harder she pushed, the harder I pushed back."

"Doesn't sound like a romance, sounds like a wrestling match," Bud said to Garret.

"Are you making fun of me?" Dave demanded.

Bud shook his head and turned his attention back to his beer.

Dave shoved Bud's shoulder. "You listen to me! Are you making fun of me?"

"Why would I want to do that?" Bud asked no one in particular. "You've already proven you're pathetic."

"What do you mean by that?" Dave asked.

Bud turned his chair around to face Dave. "I mean, I think it's pretty pathetic for a man to let an overinflated sense of himself keep him from hanging on to a woman any man would feel lucky to have love him."

Dave wrinkled up his face. "Who are you talking about, big man? Moira? What do you know about her?"

Garret was puzzled, too. What did Bud know about Moira? He had a vague recollection of seeing the two of them talking after the quarter finals game, but Bud was normally so awkward around women Garret hadn't given the conversation a second thought.

Now Bud stood, looming over Dave. "You aren't fit to kiss Moira Stapleton's boots," he declared.

Dave's face turned the color of a pickled beet. Garret rose and tried to insert himself between the two. "Steady on, mates," he said.

Dave turned to him. "You stay out of this. That bitch you're dating started all this, with her man-taming crap. Moira was a great girl before her head got filled with that nonsense."

A red fog clouded Garret's vision. "Who are you calling a bitch?" he roared. Not waiting for an answer, he punched Dave in the mouth.

Dave aimed a flailing blow to the side of Garret's head, but Bud doubled him over with a punch in the gut. Then someone hit Bud in the head with a chair, and Tate and Guy joined in.

Within thirty seconds half the men in the bar were battling on one side or the other. Other patrons were running for the exits and the bartender was shouting at someone to call the police.

By the time the cops showed up everything had pretty much ended. Friends of the combatants on either side had separated them and the bartender was handing out ice and damp towels. Garret took a collection among the players to pay for any damage, then bought a round of drinks for the house.

"What's going on here?" a baby-faced officer demanded as he and four others poured into the now-quiet saloon.

"Just a friendly difference of opinion," Garret said, dabbing at the blood on his cheek. "Everything's right as rain now."

The cop surveyed the mess of shattered chairs and spilled drinks around them, then turned to the bartender. "Do you want to press charges?"

The man shook his head. "Nah. They paid for the damages. No harm done."

The cops looked at each other and shrugged, then left.

"You want another beer?" Bud asked Garret.

He shook his head and settled into a chair once more. "So are you dating Moira now?" he asked.

Bud flushed. "We've had coffee. We're talking."

"But not dating?"

"I'm thinking about asking her out." He glanced at Garret. "What do you think? Do you think she'll go out with me?"

"Only one way to find out, mate." He settled back in his chair, the gloom that had been his constant companion of late creeping back in. "What you said back there, about a man letting an inflated opinion of himself get in the way of love. Were you talking about me?" he asked.

Bud looked surprised. "No. Why would you think that?"

"Because I think you're right. Maybe I haven't been fair to Rachel." He rested his chin in his hand and sighed. "Trouble is, I don't know what to do about it."

"You could call her up."

"And say what? It's not like she's going to stop being the Man Tamer on my say-so."

"I thought you said that didn't matter to you."

"I guess I lied." It wasn't what Rachel did for a living that bothered him as much as the idea that she couldn't love all of him, the way he loved her. He wanted her on his terms, but what if that meant he couldn't have her at all?

15

Farewell to the Man Tamer
This is my final column and I'd like to thank all
the readers who've written to me and supported
the column. I'm moving on to new, exciting
ventures. I'm wishing you all the very best of
luck with your relationships. I leave you with one
parting word of advice: love and respect are the
two most important qualities in a relationship.
You can't really have one without the other. You
can overlook a lot for the sake of those two things.
Take it from someone who learned the hard way.

NOTHING LIKE A DRIVE in the country to relax a man, Garret
thought as he roared down a flat, straight stretch of
highway west of Dallas. A hot wind blew in the open
windows of the truck, and Barney sat in the passenger seat,
head out the window, tail whipping excitedly as he took
in all the sights and smells. Garret inhaled the scent of
stockyards and cotton fields and could almost imagine he
was back home in Canberra. Except that instead of being
on the lookout for kangaroos who might hop into the
roadway, here he had to watch for deer and armadillos.

He switched on the radio and turned it up, searching for a country station. A sad song about cheating, drinking or losing love would fit well with his mood right now. Bud's words about letting his inflated opinion of himself get in the way of love nagged at him. He didn't think of himself as arrogant. What man wouldn't have been angry about that bet?

But when he thought of how things had been between him and Rachel, he couldn't see any manipulation in her actions. She'd behaved pretty much like any woman would—better than most, even. She'd attended his games and cheered him on, even though she'd admitted she'd never enjoyed sports before. She'd learned to play poker and even gotten along with Barney.

He could see now she was only being honest when she'd said she'd initially thought he wasn't her type; he could have originally said the same about her. She'd struck him as a finicky, high-brow, high-maintenance woman. And maybe she was all those things, but for him she'd been willing to change.

What was so unreasonable about her expecting him to change a little to please her, as well? He swore softly and hit his hand on the steering wheel, startling Barney. "I've been a big sodding fool," he told the dog. Was it too late to hope for a second chance?

"In local entertainment news, popular *Belinda* magazine columnist Rachel Westover, aka 'The Man Tamer' has resigned her position with the magazine, effective immediately," a woman's perky voice announced over the radio. "No word yet on Ms. Westover's plans."

At the sound of Rachel's name, Garret slammed on his brakes. He threw out his arm to keep Barney from flying off the seat and guided the truck to a stop on the side of the road. "Did you hear that?" he asked the dog. "She quit her job."

Barney's tongue lolled and he wagged his tail.

"You don't have any idea what I'm talking about, do you, old boy?" Garret asked, scratching the dog behind one ear. Had Rachel quit because of him? Or had Denton fired her? Because she'd refused to stop dating him? He scowled at the radio. If Denton *had* fired Rachel, he was going to wish he'd never met Wild Man Kelly.

He put the truck in gear and did a U-turn in the deserted road. Then he pushed the gas pedal to the floor and headed back to Dallas. Maybe he and Rachel weren't an item anymore, but he wasn't going to stand for her losing her job because of him.

On the outskirts of Dallas, Barney began to bark. Garret looked in the mirror and saw the blue-and-white strobe of a police car fast approaching. Groaning, he pulled over to the side of the road.

A female officer approached. She wore her long blond hair in a ponytail and he probably would have thought she was pretty if she'd had a more pleasant expression on her face. "Sir, do you know how fast you were going?" she asked.

"About ninety, I'd wager." Garret tried for a friendly smile. "I'm in a bit of a rush."

"May I see your license, registration and proof of insurance, please?"

Garret handed over the required paperwork. "I know I should slow down," he said. "But I heard something on the radio that upset me."

"Whatever it was, it couldn't be worth risking an accident." The officer didn't look up from her clipboard.

"I'm sure you're right. Guess I'm just one of those guys who acts without thinking sometimes." For instance, when he'd dumped Rachel without giving her a chance to explain her actions.

"I'll be back in just a moment, Mr. Kelly," she said.

Garret watched in the mirror as the cop walked back to her cruiser. Even the mannish pants and boots she wore couldn't make her walk like a guy, which was something to be thankful for, he supposed.

Barney whined and scooted closer. "It's okay, boy," Garret said as he patted the dog. "We'll collect our ticket and be on our way."

Barney barked again. When Garret looked up, he saw the officer hurrying toward him. "You're Wild Man Kelly," she said when she reached the truck.

"That would be me." Garret relaxed a little. If this cop was a fan, maybe he could get out of the ticket.

"I watched the semi-final playoff game the other night," the cop said. She shook her head. "What was with all the penalties? You spent more time in the box than you did on the floor."

Garret sank lower in the seat. "Guess I got a tad carried away," he muttered.

"They should have carried *you* away." She angled the clipboard toward him. "Sign here, please."

He scrawled his signature at the bottom of the form. She lowered her sunglasses and gave him a hard look. "I heard you used to date Rachel Westover."

"Yeah." Did the whole world know his private business now?

"I'm a real fan of her column."

"The Man Tamer." Figured.

"Guess she wasn't interested in a man who couldn't control his temper." She tore off the ticket and handed it to him. "Payment instructions are on the back. Have a nice day."

Right. His day so far was just peachy. He started the truck and slowly turned onto the highway. He waited until the cop was out of sight before he said to Barney, "How is it that a woman can lie to me and use me for her own personal gain, and yet now that we're split up, I feel like the real bastard in this whole mess?" Had all those weeks with the Man Tamer turned him into a wuss, or was guilt another symptom of True Love?

RACHEL HAD NEVER imagined that leaving her job at *Belinda* magazine would be so hard. Not emotionally wrenching—she was too excited for that. But *physically* impossible. She tugged harder on the potted philodendron that had decorated her desk. "Let go," she said to the man clinging to the other side of the pot. "I have to finish packing."

"Rachel, you can't leave." Denton Morrison refused to release his grip on the pot. "I'll give you a raise."

"It's too late." She let go of the planter and Denton

crashed back into the side of her cubicle, the plant hugged to his chest.

He straightened and set the plant on the corner of the desk, and brushed potting soil off the front of his Brooks Brothers suit. "You are aware that your contract doesn't allow you to take the Man Tamer name or concept with you when you leave," he said.

She tossed a spare makeup bag, extra shoes and a first-aid kit into a cardboard box. "I'm aware of that." Although considering how *she* had come up with the name and developed the concept herself, what made Denton think he could own it? Not that it mattered to her anymore.

"You're upset about Garret, aren't you?" Denton said. "I can understand that. Maybe I can help. I have a lot of influence with him. I could ask him to start dating you again."

"No!" She stared at Denton, horrified. "You can't *make* him want to date me."

"Why not? I can tell him I've decided to revive the whole Man Tamer versus Wild Man publicity campaign. It's in his contract that he has to promote the team."

"This isn't about the team. And I won't have my personal life turned into some publicity stunt." She tossed a stack of files into the box. "You've done enough damage already."

"You didn't mind the publicity angle when I first suggested it." He leaned back against her desk and crossed his arms. "Back then you were eager to play along."

That was before my heart got involved, she thought.

Falling in love with Garret had changed the way she thought about everything. "I'm not interested any-more," she said.

"In Garret or in the television show? I still have to pay up on my bet."

"Either one." At least not the Man Tamer television show. As for Garret—well, it would be a long time before she was ready to even think about another man in her life. "I've had a better offer," she said.

"Found another guy so soon?" Denton smirked. "So much for true love."

"Not another man." She dropped a stack of note-books into the box and sealed it up with tape. "Another television show."

"What?" Denton leaped up, wild-eyed. "What are you talking about? You can't do this to me. I'll sue."

She looked at him, trying hard not to laugh. The man was pacing the office, waving his hands in the air, prac-tically hyperventilating. If she'd known telling Denton her plans would be this much fun, she might have dropped the bomb sooner.

"You can't sue," she said. "This is a completely new show. It has nothing to do with my work here at the magazine."

"Except that this magazine made you what you are today." Denton stopped pacing and faced her. "You owe me some loyalty."

"I'll be sure to thank you in my Daytime Emmy acceptance speech." She picked up the box and squeezed past him. "I really have to go now. I have a lot to do."

"You can't just leave me like this."

"My last column is on your desk." She glanced back at the philodendron. "And you can keep the plant. As a keepsake."

He was still standing by the desk, openmouthed, when she walked out the door. She couldn't hold back a smile as she strode toward the elevator to the lobby. Who knew leaving this place could feel so good? Yes, she was taking a real gamble with her career, but it felt like a step in the right direction.

If only her personal life was in as great a shape.

When she stepped off the elevator in the lobby, she collided with something big, solid…and warm. Clutching the packing box to her chest, she looked up into familiar blue eyes. "Garret! What are you doing here?"

His arms around her were so familiar and comfortable. And he seemed in no hurry to release her. "What's all this about you quitting your job?" he asked.

"How did you know about that?"

"I heard it on the radio." He did finally ease his hold on her and stepped back. "What's going on?"

"The radio! Malcolm must be trying to build interest for my new television show." That was the trouble with working in the media. Secrets were almost impossible to keep. She shifted the box in her arms. "He could have at least waited until I had my office packed."

"Let me take that." Garret relieved her of the box. "So you're getting the television spot you wanted. I guess you convinced Denton to pay up on the bet."

The coldness of his expression made her heart ache.

"It's not like that," she said. "This has nothing to do with that awful bet."

"Let me put this in your car." He started across the lobby and she had no choice but to follow.

"Garret, just listen to me, please," she said.

He waited until they reached her car before he spoke. He set the box on the hood and turned to her. "That's why I came here. To listen. So start talking."

Where to begin? She hugged her arms across her stomach and looked around the parking lot—anywhere but at the man in front of her. "I've had a lot of time to think this past couple of weeks," she said.

"Yeah. Me, too."

The regret she thought she heard in his voice gave her hope. "I promise you, Garret, I never intentionally set out to hurt you. I—I guess I just wasn't thinking clearly when I agreed to that bet with Denton. I've wanted my own television show for so long and I saw this as a sure way to get it. I wasn't considering anything beyond that."

She glanced at him, but his expression hadn't softened any. "But you really thought I needed 'taming'?" he asked.

The hard edge to his voice made her wince. "I didn't really know you, then. And I'll admit I had a pretty unrealistic picture of what a relationship between a man and a woman should be." She met his gaze and held it. "What seemed like faults to me at first weren't nearly as big as I imagined once I really got to know you." She managed a shaky smile. "I think I finally know what they mean when they say 'love is blind.'"

"I know all about acting before I think." He shoved

his hands into his pockets and studied the pavement between his feet. "Listen—I owe you an apology. That's what I really came here to say today. I stormed off the night of your sister's big charity ball without giving you a chance to tell me your side of things."

"And now that you've heard my side, what do you think?" She hugged herself more tightly. Could he hear how loudly her heart was pounding?

He blew out a breath. "I don't know. I mean, there's still the whole man-taming thing."

"I'm done with man taming. You or anyone else."

"What about your television show?"

"It's not about man taming." She grinned, excitement over this new project overcoming even her distress over their future. "When I realized what a mess man taming had made of my life—and maybe other lives, as well— I wanted to use what I'd learned to help others. I knew Denton would never listen to me, so I went to his chief competitor, Malcolm Rylander, of station KXAM, and proposed a new kind of show to him."

"What kind of show?"

"This show is for couples, to teach them to work together to bring out the best in each other. Malcolm loved it." Of course, he would have loved anything that would allow him to get the best of Denton, but she was sure she could make this show a hit.

"We certainly brought out the best in each other." Garret smiled and pulled her into his arms. "Whatever your original intentions, you did take a few rough edges off this wild man—and helped make me a better person. And I like to think I did the same for you."

"You did." She smiled up at him, so full of happiness she might have floated away if he hadn't held her tightly. "Am I forgiven now?"

"You're forgiven." He kissed her forehead. "Think you can forgive me?"

"I forgive you." She stood on tiptoe and kissed him on the mouth, sealing the bargain between them. "There's only one other thing," she said when they parted at last.

"What's that?"

"I need a co-host for my show," she said. "Someone who can share the man's point of view. Someone talented. Handsome. Understanding. Intelligent."

He looked thoughtful. "I might know the man for the job. But don't you think it would be better if the show's hosts were a married couple? A pair who could, as one of your man-taming principles urged—teach by example?"

She gripped his arm, steadying herself. Did she dare trust her hearing? "What are you suggesting?" she asked warily.

His eyes met hers, his gaze steady and sober. "I'm asking you to marry me. I'm even willing to clean up my apartment and let you buy me more clothes if you'll agree to be my wife."

She swallowed hard, determined not to burst into messy tears or hysterical shouting, though she felt close to doing both. "And I'll agree to continue to attend lacrosse games and overlook your bizarre dietary habits and love of sports." She gave him a wobbly smile. "We'll prove that compromise in love can be a good thing for both partners," she said.

He grinned. "Have you tamed the Wild Man, or has the Wild Man brought out the more adventurous side of you?"

"A little of both, maybe." She laughed, no longer able to contain her joy. "We may have to find new nicknames."

"How about husband and wife?"

"Mmm. I like the sound of it already." Then they both stopped talking and let their kisses say everything else they needed to say.

* * * * *

*Let three tantalising sexy men into your
life this summer in…*

TALL, DARK…AND DANGEROUSLY HOT!,

*Mills & Boon® Blaze®'s sizzling new mini-series.
The passion begins in May 2008 with*
The PI
by Cara Summers.

Turn the page for a sneak preview!

The PI

by

Cara Summers

Thursday, August 27—near midnight

IN THE TOWER ROOM on the top floor of her house, Cass Angelis sat at her rosewood desk and prepared to see the future.

Laurel leaves burned in a glass bowl, candlelight flickered on the walls and the music of Yolanda Kondonassis, the Greek harpist, flowed around her. Her ability as a seer came as naturally to Cass as gardening or cooking came to other women. In her younger years, she'd used her abilities to help anyone who came to her. It was only after her husband Demetrius's death that she'd begun to charge for her services, and over the last eighteen years, she'd built up enough of a reputation in the San Francisco area to make a comfortable living.

But tonight she had no client. Tonight her concern was for her family. Her son, Dino, who was serving his country in the Navy, her nephews, Nik, Theo and Kit, and her niece, Philly—she wasn't sure which one or ones the Fates would offer choices to. All she was sure of was that choices would be offered this weekend. The small china clock on the mantel read two minutes to midnight—the witching hour. Not that Cass was a witch, not by a long shot. She couldn't have whipped up a spell to save her life. But she did have insights into what the Fates might weave into a person's future.

Might weave because it was always up to the individual to embrace or try to escape their destiny.

Her gift of sight had been inherited from her great-grandmother, Ariel Andropoulis, who'd claimed that her powers could be traced all the way back to Apollo's Oracle at Delphi. Cass liked to believe that was true. On occasions like tonight she even burned laurel leaves the way Apollo's priestesses had. But the only thing she was certain of was that psychic powers ran in her family, especially in the females.

Her sister had possessed the ability to "see," too, and although Cass knew that Penelope had passed it on in some form to all four of her children, it was only Philly who acknowledged and used her gift.

Cass glanced at the latest family portrait that her nephews and niece had given her for her birthday last month. She was in the same chair she sat in now. Her brother-in-law Spiro stood to her left. Philly sat on the arm of the chair and Nik, Theo and Kit stood behind and to her right. Dino hadn't been there for the photo. Currently, he was stationed in the Gulf. All of the Angelis men loved the sea, but Dino had been most susceptible to its lure. From when he was a little boy, she'd sensed that one day he would leave, so she hadn't been surprised when he'd applied to Annapolis.

Cass continued to study the family photo. The Angelis men were all beautiful—tall, dark and handsome, just as her husband, Demetrius, had been and, for just a moment, she allowed herself to drift backward to the past.

When she and Penelope had graduated from high

school, their father had taken them to Greece. He'd intended to put them in touch with their heritage, but she and Penelope had "known" that the visit to Greece would offer them much more.

Cass's mind filled with images of Ionic columns, marble statues and theatres built into sloping hillsides. Although she and Penelope had been fascinated by the history, the culture and the literature of the country, it had been the sea that had drawn them the most. They'd dragged their father to just about every fishing village along the coast, and it had been in one of them that they'd met Spiro and Demetrius Angelis.

For both her sister and herself, it had been a case of love at first sight. Still, Cass wasn't certain that she and Penelope would have had the courage to grab what the Fates had offered them. Luckily, the two Angelis brothers had taken the decision out of their hands by following them back to San Francisco. With her father's help, they'd opened their own restaurant, The Poseidon. For a time, Cass had known what it was like to love and be truly loved in return.

With a sigh, she shifted her gaze to a picture of Demetrius. She knew all too well that the Fates were fickle. What they gave could be snatched away at any time, but even in the worst of times, they offered unexpected gifts.

Spiro, his children and Dino had been her family since that day nearly eighteen years ago when Demetrius and Penelope had lost their lives in a boating accident. Nik, her oldest nephew, had been twelve, the same age as Dino. Theo had been eleven, Kit ten and little Philly had been only four. Spiro had been left with the restaurant to run all on his own. So her father had invited them all to move into his house, and she'd taken over the job of raising Penelope's and Spiro's children along with her son.

Cass smiled. Her sadness had been followed by unexpected joy, as she'd come to look upon Penelope's children as her own. At some point in the wink of time, the Angelis boys had become men. Her gaze returned to the photo of her husband Demetrius. And at least one of them was about to find the love of his life just as she had.

Maybe that was why she'd been thinking of Demetrius. It would happen this weekend—if they chose to take what the Fates offered them.

The first stroke of midnight brought Cass out of her reverie. Taking a deep breath, she put away the odd sense of loneliness that she'd been feeling lately and lifted her crystals. Light from a full moon streamed through tall, narrow windows and the milky mist in the faceted jewels began to swirl. She often saw things more clearly at that magic moment when one day gave way to the next. When the clock chimed again, the shadows in the stones broke into colors—a rainbow of them. They warmed her palms, and slowly, colors shifted, parted, then bled into one another until an image formed in her mind—a young woman, small and blonde with bottle-green eyes. And she was racing down a shadowed flight of stairs. In a holy place? Before Cass could get a real sense of the surroundings or the circumstances, the colors shifted again, and this time it was Kit, her youngest nephew, she saw. The young woman was at his side and they were both running through the darkness. This time she sensed danger.

Closing her eyes, Cass tried to see beyond the images to what they meant. A damsel in distress for Kit. The Fates had chosen wisely, she thought. Her youngest nephew, the dreamer, had always had an errant-knight streak in him.

Even as joy streamed through her, her heart squeezed a bit. Kit would be the first of her children to meet the woman he was fated for. From the time he was small, Kit had always been insatiably curious, and that characteristic had often gotten him into scrapes. It had also shaped him for his future careers as a P.I. and a crime-fiction writer. Her lips curved slightly. The boy just couldn't resist solving puzzles. Yes, a damsel in distress would do very well.

Shifting her attention back to the swirling colors in the crystals, Cass moved them in her hands and watched the rainbows grow darker and darker until everything was gray. Suddenly, a flash of fire knifed through the darkness. Cass's heart chilled and her stomach tightened with fear. What she saw was money, guns and blood. What she sensed was greed, envy and death.

The crystals burned now against her skin. But she kept her gaze steady. Colors flashed again, shattering the darkness. And she sensed the love—passionate and true.

Would it be enough to protect her Kit and the woman the Fates had chosen for him?

0408/14

MILLS & BOON

Blaze

On sale 2nd May 2008

THE PI
by Cara Summers

Tall, Dark...and Dangerously Sexy

PI Kit Angelis is stunned when a woman walks into his office, covered in blood and with no idea of who she is. She's also sinfully sexy, making it hard for Kit to keep his mind on the mystery...

RELEASE
by Jo Leigh

Seth Turner is a soldier without a battle. Secreted in a safe house with gorgeous Dr Harper Douglas, can he fight the heated sexual attraction escalating between them?

LETTING LOOSE!
by Mara Fox

Tina Henderson knows exactly what she needs. A wild night with a stripper will make her forget all about Tyler Walden. Only there's more to 'The Bandit' than meets the eye...

NO RULES
by Shannon Hollis

Are the *Laws of Seduction* the latest dating fad...or a blueprint for murder? Along with her sexy partner, Cooper Maxwell, Joanna MacPherson is going to find out. But the dangerous investigation uncovers a lot more than they bargained for...

Celebrate 100 years of pure reading pleasure with Mills & Boon®

To mark our centenary, each month we're publishing a special 100th Birthday Edition. These celebratory editions are packed with extra features and include a FREE bonus story.

Plus, starting in February you'll have the chance to enter a fabulous monthly prize draw. See 100th Birthday Edition books for details.

Now that's worth celebrating!

15th February 2008

Raintree: Inferno by Linda Howard
Includes FREE bonus story Loving Evangeline
A double dose of Linda Howard's heady mix of passion and adventure

4th April 2008

The Guardian's Forbidden Mistress by Miranda Lee
Includes FREE bonus story The Magnate's Mistress
Two glamorous and sensual reads from favourite author Miranda Lee!

2nd May 2008

The Last Rake in London by Nicola Cornick
Includes FREE bonus story The Notorious Lord
Lose yourself in two tales of high society and rakish seduction!

Look for Mills & Boon 100th Birthday Editions at your favourite bookseller or visit
www.millsandboon.co.uk

2 FREE

BOOKS AND A SURPRISE GIFT!

We would like to take this opportunity to thank you for reading this Mills & Boon® book by offering you the chance to take TWO more specially selected titles from the Superromance series absolutely FREE! We're also making this offer to introduce you to the benefits of the Mills & Boon® Reader Service™—

- ★ **FREE home delivery**
- ★ **FREE gifts and competitions**
- ★ **FREE monthly Newsletter**
- ★ **Exclusive Reader Service offers**
- ★ **Books available before they're in the shops**

Accepting these FREE books and gift places you under no obligation to buy, you may cancel at any time, even after receiving your free shipment. Simply complete your details below and return the entire page to the address below. You don't even need a stamp!

YES! Please send me 2 free Superromance books and a surprise gift. I understand that unless you hear from me, I will receive 4 superb new titles every month for just £3.69 each, postage and packing free. I am under no obligation to purchase any books and may cancel my subscription at any time. The free books and gift will be mine to keep in any case.

U8ZED

Ms/Mrs/Miss/Mr ....Initials ....
BLOCK CAPITALS PLEASE

Surname ....

Address ....

....

....Postcode..

Send this whole page to:
UK: FREEPOST CN81, Croydon, CR9 3WZ

Offer valid in UK only and is not available to current Mills & Boon® Reader Service™ subscribers to this series. Overseas and Eire please write for details and readers in Southern Africa write to Box 3010, Pinegowie, 2123 RSA. We reserve the right to refuse an application and applicants must be aged 18 years or over. Only one application per household. Terms and prices subject to change without notice. Offer expires 30th June 2008. As a result of this application, you may receive offers from Harlequin Mills & Boon and other carefully selected companies. If you would prefer not to share in this opportunity please write to The Data Manager, PO Box 676, Richmond, TW9 1WU.

Mills & Boon® is a registered trademark owned by Harlequin Mills & Boon Limited.
The Mills & Boon® Reader Service™ is being used as a trademark.